Taffy of Torpedo Junction

A Chapel Hill Book

Taffy

of Torpedo Junction

With a New Foreword by Bland Simpson

by Nell Wise Wechter

Illustrated by Mary Walker Sparks

The University of North Carolina Press

Chapel Hill and London

First published by The University of North Carolina Press in 1996

© 1996 by Marcia Wechter Kass

New Foreword © 1996 by The University of North Carolina Press

Originally published in 1957 by John F. Blair

Manufactured in the United States of America

Library of Congress Cataloging-in-Publication Data

Wechter, Nell Wise.

Taffy of Torpedo Junction / by Nell Wise Wechter; with a new
foreword by Bland Simpson; illustrated by Mary Walker Sparks.

p. cm. "A Chapel Hill book"—2nd printed p. Summary: In
1942, thirteen-year-old Taffy, living with her grandfather on Hatteras
Island, inadvertently helps capture Nazi spies responsible for passing
information to offshore German submarines engaged in torpedoing
American ships. ISBN 0-8078-4619-8 (pbk.: alk. paper)

1. World War, 1939–1946 — North Carolina — Outer Banks —
Fiction. 2. Outer Banks (N.C.)—Fiction. [1. World War,
1939–1945 — North Carolina — Outer Banks — Fiction.
2. Hatteras Island (N.C.)—Fiction. 3. Spies —Fiction.
4. Islands —Fiction. 5. North Carolina—Fiction.]
I. Sparks, Mary Walker, ill. II. Title. 96-8050
PS3573.E283T34 1996 CIP
813'.54[Fic]— dc20 AC

04 03 02 01 8 7 6 5

To my daughter Marcia
(who never saw a burning ship)

and to Bob, my husband
(who saw many)

Contents

Foreword ix

Acknowledgments xvii

1 A Call in the Night 1

2 Shipwreck 22

3 Rescue 30

4 Ash Cans and Broken Glass 49

5 Torpedo Junction 64

6 Saboteur! 79

7 Brandy Gets Decorated 96

8 Discovery! 105

9 Danger! 110

10 Big Jens Comes Through 120

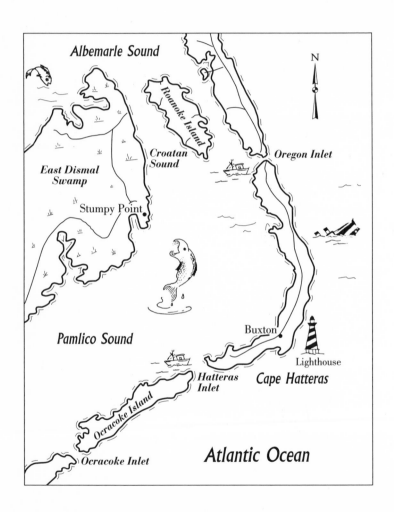

Albemarle Sound

Roanoke Island

Croatan
Sound

Oregon Inlet

East Dismal
Swamp

Stumpy Point

N

Pamlico Sound

Buxton

Lighthouse

Hatteras
Inlet

Cape Hatteras

Ocracoke Island

Ocracoke Inlet

Atlantic Ocean

Foreword

When Nell Wise Wechter wrote of her time as a teacher on North Carolina's Outer Banks during the Second World War, turning a local tomboy into fictional heroine Taffy Willis in the 1957 novel *Taffy of Torpedo Junction*, she gave our state and nation a terrific adventure story and opened a window through which we can still see clearly our Carolina coast of over a half century ago. The battle of Torpedo Junction—steady, devastating German submarine attacks on Allied shipping during the first six months of 1942—was only fifteen years past when Wechter published *Taffy*, and her slender, award-winning novel seems as fresh and straight-ahead today as it did when I first heard it.

I remember well our teacher Miss Audrey Austin reading Wechter's brand-new book aloud to our fourth grade Elizabeth City class, and how quickly and vividly Taffy and her world came to life. Miss Austin believed that, as young Carolinians, we ought to know what had gone on during the war on the Outer Banks, just a little over an hour's drive from where we lived, and with good reason — eighty-seven vessels were lost off our coast, mostly tankers and cargo ships, and most of them were sunk between January and August of 1942. Author Wechter recalled the submarines hitting a convoy of tankers one night, hearing the boom, boom, boom of the torpedoes exploding, and then "in thirty minutes it looked like day from all the ships burning." Her history was compelling, and her thirteen-year-old Taffy, who challenged the on-shore collaborator-saboteurs of the German U-boats, was every bit as attractive an adventurer as another young hero Miss Austin had been reading to us about, the boy in Walter Farley's *Black Stallion* series. And Taffy Willis was just as good riding bareback on her Banks pony as the boy was on his Arabian.

From the first page, where we found ourselves on a sandy trail through the island woods, we knew *Taffy* was *our* story. We too had played in the live oak forests and myrtle thickets, and we had longed to catch and ride those wild ponies that roamed the Banks. And all of us had seen the rippled traces of oil left by the tides at the beach, oil that periodically rose from the deep, and heard our elders speak gravely of "the sunken ships." Where Farley's books were exotic by nature, *Taffy* was all about a North Carolinian, and we knew right where she lived. Yes, Taffy was ours, all right, and she and her dangerous adventure were as good as real.

"Will war come to us, Gramp? Here? On Cape Hatteras?" Taffy asks her grandfather after they have heard the radio broadcast telling of the Japanese attack on Pearl Harbor. Indeed, war came quickly to the Outer Banks, in spades, and if this were the front line during the war, as far as we young readers and read-tos were concerned, who better to defend it than someone more or less our age? Who better than Taffy Willis on her pony, Sailor, galloping over dunes with abandon and apparently near-total independence and just brave — and reckless — enough to follow her hunches right into the lair of danger? For her nation's enemies were not only aboard the submarines that by day lay lurking on the oceanfloor of Diamond Shoals and by night rose to spot the Allied ships silhouetted against the shore lights and sink them—they were also abroad in the live oak forest around Buxton. Taffy did her duty as she saw it, she had pluck, and she was a good kid—the girls at J. C. Sawyer Elementary School all idolized her, and the boys all fell in love.

Like Taffy, nearly all of us had kin on the coast— people with names like Midyette and Etheridge, Daniels and Baum—and we were well acquainted with maritime men like Taffy's Gramp Morgan, who spoke the old *soundside* or *hightide* brogue best typified by the remark, "It'll be a hoightoide on the saoundsoide tonoight!" He talked a lot like a lot of folks we knew and were related to who began conjectures with "Oi reckon" and called outsiders "dingbatters" and "ditdots" and, when bothered by something, said they were "mommicked." Theirs is a speech still heard, with local variation, from Hatteras and Ocracoke, south to Cedar Island and Harkers Island, in coastal communities from Currituck to Carteret County and beyond.

There has been many a high tide in the fifty years since World War II and the nearly forty years since *Taffy*'s first edition. When the old ferry over Oregon Inlet from Bodie Island to Hatteras Island gave way to the arch and curve of the Herbert Bonner Bridge in 1964, what a vast change it seemed to us, for Hatteras Island had been such a world apart. Even so, because of the creation of Cape Hatteras National Seashore and, more recently, Cape Lookout National Seashore with its Core Banks shanties and fish camps, some stretches of our coast are still as isolated and wild as the world in which Taffy was living.

Millions visit our edge of the sea, whose history Wechter's novel so effectively illuminates, and there are still somber reminders of the last great global conflict and how it affected us. Many who reach Ocracoke village, on the next island below Hatteras, wander by a small cemetery in the myrtle and yaupon that holds the graves of four British seamen whose bodies washed ashore on the beach there. Reading *Taffy* now, one does so mindful that the Germans and the Japanese, our great trading partners today, were our country's mortal enemies then — and the book is an honest testament to the rigors and harsh feelings of wartime — especially among a people who felt scarcely defended and who kept a brave vigil against the constant uncertainty of what the Atlantic seas might bring them.

Yet, as full of history and sense of place and social portraiture as it is, *Taffy* is a novel, a good story first and foremost, a literary gift from a teacher, intended for young readers, each of whom would naturally yearn to be as bold a soldier as the bareback-riding heroine, who would be crazily curious as to what she was on the trail of, and who would pull for her through it all. On the shelf of Carolina writing that includes Thomas Wolfe's *Look Homeward, Angel*, Doris Betts's *The River to Pickle Beach*, Kaye Gibbons's *Ellen Foster*, and Samm-Art Williams's *Home*, *Taffy of Torpedo Junction* may seem to be the innocent among them, though Wechter gave her heroine no shortage of reality and peril—Taffy's parents lost at sea and Taffy herself the victim of ambush and attempted murder. For many of us who were still under ten back then, though, Wechter's *Taffy* and John Harden's *The Devil's Tramping Ground* were the first literary inklings that real and noteworthy things of history—and *mystery*—had occurred right in the small towns and country crossroads where we lived, and that the telling and retelling of these stories in classrooms and living rooms and around firesides at camp were no small part of what bound us together as Tar Heels, as Southerners, and as Americans. It is a good thing to go back and settle in and read and *see* Taffy again—for she, like the creations of these Carolina authors and others, is a part of who we are.

So meet her, whether for the first time or anew, on ponyback in Buxton Woods on Hatteras Island, outer reef of Pamlico Sound, last sandbar before Africa. And hats off, salute her, for she was in the war. And it is a good thing, too, in this day of our ailing rivers and sounds and fisheries, to remember what Taffy and her mullet-fishing Gramp were fighting for. Ride like the wind, Taffy Willis, and we ride with you, as we did when we were children and as our children do now. Why, by the end of the tale, we may even be able to *roide*.

Bland Simpson
Chapel Hill, North Carolina
March 1996

Acknowledgments

The author wishes to express her grateful acknowledgment and appreciation to the News Bureau of the North Carolina Department of Conservation and Development, Raleigh, N.C., for the use of photographs which helped the illustrator get a sharper vision of Cape Hatteras Island; to Mr. D. V. Meekins, Editor of the *Coastland Times*, Manteo, N.C., for permission to use the coastland map; to Miss Mary Ann Stafford, her typist, who struggled over the revision; and to Mr. L. W. Anderson, President of the Greensboro Writers, whose kindly criticism aided her immeasurably in writing the book.

Taffy of Torpedo Junction

This story is based on many events that actually happened, and the line between fact and fiction is rather thin at times. The characters are entirely fictional. Gramp Morgan and Sal Oden never existed except in the imagination of the author. Taffy and her island friends exemplify the daring courage of all the teen-age youngsters who lived in the Outer Banks of North Carolina during the dark days of World War II.

But Torpedo Junction is no legend—that long strip of treacherous shoals off Cape Hatteras, so named because of the number of ships that were torpedoed there. Perhaps, someday in the future, someone will be able to dig out the actual dates and names of those brave men and ships who offered their last devotion to their country off the Diamond Shoals—in Torpedo Junction.

I. A Call in the Night

Taffy clucked to her horse, gently pulling the left rein of the bridle. The little Banks pony, shaggy from burrs in his matted, reddish-brown mane, tossed his head as he turned off the beach and trotted down the sandy trail through Buxton woods.

"Oh, but you're a proud one this morning," Taffy said to her horse. "Reckon you're thinking of those Barbary ancestors of yours that Sir Walter Raleigh's colonists brought over. Shucks, your grandpop might have been brought over by a Portugee sailor for all you know. Anyhow, you're just an old sandfiddler like me." She grinned, showing white teeth in a face as fair as an evening sunset off the Cape. "If you want to feel proud, look at those sea oats over there, gleaming like gold on the dunes. Reckon the fall of the year has really come to the island for sure."

Taffy looked down at her faded blue shirt and jeans, one leg rolled to her knees, the other flapping against the wind, and at her bare feet, as brown as berries. She sighed, thinking of the winter ahead— the time when she would have to encase her brown feet in shoe leather again. "Oh, well," she shrugged as the pony jounced over a knoll of sand in the trail, "what has to be, has to be. Sailor, we might as well ride down the back road. 'Tisn't mail time yet. Sure hope Gramp gets his check this morning."

Horse and rider passed through a thicket of pines under which stood hundreds of twisted yaupon bushes and green palmettos. Nowhere in the thicket could she see a tree or shrub whose leaves had turned brown or yellow. The Gulf Stream kept the North Carolina Banks subtropical all the year, as a general rule. Occasionally, though, a hard north-easter would whip up a storm that would chill the island with a wintry blast. Taffy shivered, thinking how wonderful it would be to have a thick blanket of white snow just once. "I reckon that's too much to wish for," she thought, "but it would be nice."

The horse came to the end of the thicket. Taffy stopped the pony and stared at the big old gabled house sitting on a high sand knoll in the edge of the woods. The round wooden tower always made her feel as if Bluebeard were lurking somewhere close by to snatch her, lock her up in the tower, and finally have her head chopped off. She shuddered deliciously, relishing the blood and thunder of the old fairy tale. She wondered, as she had dozens of times in the past, why in the world the old tower was built and what it was used for now. As usual, the windows were boarded up and there was no appearance of life around the place. The big sign, NO TRESPASSING, still hung on the high board fence. The gate was securely padlocked. The place had always fascinated her, ever since she could remember. Like all the Buxton folk, however, she respected the NO TRESPASSING sign and kept her distance, wondering why the "furriners" from Baltimore were so unfriendly. She remembered hearing that some Kinnakeet boys had been peppered with bird shot one night when they had attempted to climb over the high fence.

Taffy had seen one of the Snyder sons that day three years ago when they took over the old Wollinson place. "He sure was sassy-looking too," she remembered. "Reckon that's how all Yankees look, though," she giggled to herself.

Sailor snorted at a sand fly. "Steady, boy," she said to the pony, gently rubbing his flank where the fly had bitten. She squinted against the sun. "Seems like there's something a little different looking about the place this morning, but I can't figure what. Wish I could go inside and look at all the fine things they must have in there," she thought wistfully.

The brief moment of wistfulness went as quickly as it came. She wheeled Sailor around and galloped down the sandy trail, forgetting the whole business in her desire for Gramp's check to be in the day's mail. That was the real important thing. So much depended on the small stipend which Gramp received each month from the government. So much depended on its not being late in arriving.

She jumped down from the pony and threw his reins over the scrawny limb of a scrub oak which stood near the back of the post office. She could see the elderly postmistress sorting the mail.

"Did Gramp's pension check come, Miz Oden?" she asked in a sprightly, chipper voice over the high counter.

Mrs. Oden turned around from her mail-sorting and sternly fixed her eye on the freckled face peering over the counter.

"Taffy, ain't Oi told you and told you not to bother me mornin's till Oi git the mail put up? You interfere with government business when you do. Naow run along. You'll see the 'Mail's Up' soign when Oi get through."

"Yessum," the girl said meekly, sitting down on the steps where she began to worry the sand around with her brown, bare feet. It seemed as if the postmistress had been crotchety to her ever since she could remember. Always had something sharp or Biblical to say to her about her thoughtlessness or criticised Gramp for letting her "run wild as a Banks pony." Taffy didn't mind about herself, but it made her plum mad all over to have anyone speak ill of Gramp. Gramp was her family. All she had. And she loved him devotedly. No matter if he was old and peculiar. No matter if they did live in a fishing shack on the beach close to the big breakers of the ocean.

And no matter if they were poor and didn't have electric lights and things like most of the islanders. They were happy.

Tossing the mane of red-gold hair out of her eyes, Taffy stood up and peered into the post office door. The sign still wasn't up. She sighed and walked over to Mrs. Oden's duck pen.

"Wish I had a cold biscuit to toss to you," she told the quacking ducks. "But I reckon Miz Oden would have a hissy and think I was trying to poison you." The big mallard drake waddled up close and quacked harder.

Just then several cars and a coast guard jeep drove up. Mail time saw much activity around the post office. Taffy sauntered over to where Sailor was tied. He lifted his head and snorted.

"Steady, boy," Taffy patted him. "That jeep isn't going to hurt you." The new-fangled vehicles that had made their advent on the island since the war started always seemed to upset Sailor. Taffy thought of the day she had ridden the pony over a dune and had met a jeep in an almost-head-on collision. Ever since that day Sailor had hated jeeps.

"Looks like the mail must be up by the way folks

are going in," Taffy thought. "Reckon I'll have to wait till old Miz Oden has given all the others their mail before she waits on me. Gee whiz, I hope Gramp's check comes. We sure are short on rations."

People who had lockboxes got their mail and began leaving.

"Hi, Taffy," Big Jens of the DF Station called. "Your Gramp got any fresh mullet today?"

"Yes, sir," Taffy hollered back. "Fresh caught less than two hours ago."

"Tell him I want half a dozen big ones. I'll be down to get them in about an hour."

"Yes, sir."

Big Jens was chief warrant officer in charge of the Coast Guard Direction Finder Station on Cape Hatteras island. He had been the commanding officer for nearly two years and had bought mullet from Gramp Morgan ever since he came to the island. Taffy liked the big Norwegian. She also liked his wife, who was kind and motherly and always had time to say something happy or pleasant. Twice, she remembered, Mrs. Jens had brought them lemon pies. It was a wonder, too, the chief's wife could spare two whole pies when sugar was rationed so closely. But best of all, she liked Kenny Jens, the chief's fourteen-year-old son. He wasn't stuck up like a lot of the young tourists who came to the island before the war. He was in Taffy's class at the village school.

Taffy walked back to the post office door. "Any mail, Miz Oden?"

"Yes, yer Gramp's check come," the old lady snapped. "Reckon you'll waste half of it boyin' foolish mess at the store. Oi can't see for the loife of me whoy your Gramp lets you do it. Reckon he's jest soft in the head. Else he'd of put you in a foundlin' home when yer pa and ma got drownded. Oi ain't got no patience with an old man troyin' to raise a young girl. Just ain't fittin'. Reckon there's Scripture agin it!" Mrs. Oden snorted.

"You leave my Gramp alone." Taffy gritted her teeth, trying to hold back the salt tears that ran down her cheeks. "He's the best Gramp in the world." She grabbed the letter and ran to her horse, choking down the big, angry sob that welled in her throat. "Giddap, Sailor." She slapped him on the rump. "Giddap, boy."

Down the sandy trail they went flying, past the

schoolhouse and the Methodist church to where the road turned toward the beach. They took the sand fences like a bird on the wing, Taffy's red-gold hair spreading out behind her like a sail, the wind drying her tears.

In a matter of minutes Taffy rode up to the shack she called home. Gramp Morgan was squatted under a scrub oak mending his mullet net.

"Got it, Gramp," she called exultantly.

"Course you got it," Gramp told her. "This here was the day to get it—second day of the month always is. Now you can go boy that canned milk and package of sugar and bake them little cakes you've been pantin' to make."

"Old Miz Oden was cantankerous again," Taffy sniffed. "Said you ought to have put me in a foundling home when my mom and pop got lost."

"Looks loike Sal Oden would have enough to do withaout tendin' everybody else's business," Gramp fumed. "Her tongue must be a mixture of adder's venom and carbolic acid. But don't you let her worry you none, girlie. One of these days Oi'm going to tell her a piece of moy moind. Confabbin' old busybody! Get me a pencil. Oi'll endorse this here check and you can run daown to the store and get the things Oi wrote on the list."

In a jiffy Taffy was off again, she and Sailor flying over the level beach toward the village of Buxton.

Gramp continued to mend his net. His wrinkled old face was set in stern lines. "Reckon lots of folks criticoise me for troyin' to raise Taffy," he said to himself. "Maybe it moight of been better if Oi'd put her in an orphan home. But she's happy. She's broight as a new silver dollar, and as independent as they come." He thought of that bleak February morning ten years before when Taffy's parents had capsized in the ocean during a sudden storm while they were fishing off the Cape. He remembered how Jane, Taffy's mother, had cautioned him that morning:

"Keep a sharp watch on Taffy, Pop. You know haow quick a three-year-old youngun can get into trouble. Don't let her aout of your soight for a minute, else she'll scamper into them ocean breakers and be drownded before you know it. Me and Tom'll be back by four o'clock. There's a pot of hominy beans on the stove a-cookin' and pone bread in the oven."

"Don't you fret none abaout Taffy. Oi'll take care

of her," Gramp promised. He always did look after his granddaughter when Tom and Jane went blue fishing. About two o'clock that day a sudden storm made up off the Cape. It lasted for two days. The coast guard found Tom's boat washed up on the beach close to Hatteras Inlet. Taffy's parents were never found. Gramp Morgan kept Taffy and raised her in his own fashion. Now she was thirteen. If she did both a boy's and a girl's work, she never complained, accepting it as her lot and as a help to her grandfather, who had long ago passed his seventieth birthday. If she was free as the birds to roam the beach, Gramp was glad. He wanted her to be independent and unafraid. So much the better for her, he thought, when she went away to college. For Gramp was determined that Taffy should get a college education. He thought of the lard tin he had buried in the sand out back of the lean-to on the shack. Not a soul but him and his Maker knew about that buried tin. All the time that Taffy had been growing up, he had been putting money into that container. Whenever he sold a mess of mullets or a bucket of scallops, he'd salt away the silver in the buried tin. He chuckled, thinking that the lard can must be getting pretty heavy by now. In his big budget trunk, in the leather wallet with his retirement papers from the life saving service, he had put a piece of paper telling Taffy about the money if he should suddenly pass away.

The stern lines smoothed from his face as he spied his granddaughter and Sailor coming over the sand dunes.

"She's a sproightly youngun," he mused contentedly. "Such a blessin' to me in moy old age. The Lord will provoide," he mumbled reverently. "Reckon we'll get along all roight for a whoile yet, in spoite of Sal Oden's perdictions!"

While Taffy was stowing away the purchases from the store, Big Jens came after the mullets.

"As noice fish as Oi've caught in a month," Gramp bragged, putting the fat mullets into Big Jens' pail.

"Sure are, Gramp," the chief agreed. "Reckon you're going to have to stop fishing at night from now on, though. Government regulations. Can't have any lights showing on or near the beach."

"Naow, can you beat that?" Gramp fussed. "Same as it was in 1918. Looks loike they stir up a new war abaout every twenty-foive years or so."

"The enemy is more daring and bolder than he was in the first World War, Gramp. It's worse this time."

"Won't never forget the day that German submarine sunk the loightship off Doiamond Shoals," Gramp reminisced. "Saounded loike the whole Atlantic was gettin' blowed up. Loike to have cost some of our Cape boys their loives, too. Them that was crewmen on the loightship."

"You're going to have to put some black cloth over your windows at night, Gramp. Fix them well, so that your light won't show out on the beach. Be sure to tell Taffy about it. All the beaches down this way have been put under a stiff blackout."

"You know a lot more than you're tellin', Big Jens," Gramp said seriously. "Saounds loike the enemy moight be interested in these here parts."

"Could be. Don't be surprised if you see coast guardsmen patrolling this beach day and night from now on. They might even have dogs with them. No matter what you see or hear out here, Gramp, remember to keep quiet. Any loose talk might give comfort and aid to an enemy who might be hanging around somewhere unexpected like."

"You ain't got to learn your grandma to suck eggs, Big Jens." Gramp drew himself up. "Reckon Oi hate them danged Nazis as much as anybody. But it plain makes me mad to have to give up moy noight fishin'. Whoy, that's when the fish run best, hang it all!"

"Nevertheless, that's an order, Gramp. And don't forget about blacking out your windows. Be sure no light shines out. You're very close to the ocean out here on the point of the Cape."

Taffy had her ear glued to the door crack. Tinkles of danger ran thrillingly up and down her spine. She knew Big Jens had warned Gramp that trouble might be lurking, and not too far away either — danger that was real as the sea oats growing by the window. Hadn't Miss White, the teacher at school, told them how the war had started; how the Nazis and Fascists wanted to grasp all the power and riches of the world; how they were overrunning the small countries of Europe; and worst of all, how cruelly the enemy soldiers were treating the people they took as prisoners. It made her blood boil to think of the horrible things that were happening across the sea. But now, she knew, just as sure as she was Taffy Undine Willis, that somehow or other some of that danger had crossed the ocean to the American side. Blackouts, patrolmen, and trained dogs coming to the island? It was unheard of. What could it mean? What was there on these lonely sand strips of the Outer Banks that the enemy wanted? For some reason or other, the old, boarded-up house on the sand knoll in the woods flashed through her mind. She tried for a moment to think what it was that had looked different about it that morning. She had it! It was something that looked like an old ladder set up on the roof. That's what it was. "Reckon the Snyders are going to clean out their chimney," she thought, dismissing it from her mind as she watched Big Jens stow his pail of mullets into the back of the jeep.

"And Gramp," Big Jens called, "if you see or hear anything suspicious out here, send Taffy on Sailor to the DF Station as fast as she can get there."

"Aye, and that Oi will," Gramp promised.

Big Jens got into the jeep and swung down the beach toward the Station.

"Gramp, what kind of place is the DF Station?" Taffy whisked breathlessly out the door to the tree where her grandfather was again mending his net.

"Don't roightly know, Taffy," Gramp told her, looking at her curiously. "Seems loike Oi heard tell that it's got radio equipment that sends bearin's to ships when they call in askin' directions. Back some years ago, when the navy operated the station, folks was allowed to go in and visit. Oi've never been in there. Seems loike Oi heard the coast guard had put in some koind of new-fangled machinery since they took over. Radar or somethin'. Don't know nothin' abaout it. And don't you go askin' them coast guard boys no questions neither. What we don't know won't hurt us none. Specially naow that it's war-toime. Besoides, them station boys ain't supposed to do no talkin'. You heard what Big Jens said. Oi know you was eavesdroppin'."

"Radio equipment," Taffy exclaimed. "That's it. That's exactly it!"

"Whatever are you talkin' abaout, child?" Gramp asked her. "Your oyes are lit up loike burnt holes in a blanket."

"Oh, Gramp, don't you see? Can't you see what Big Jens was trying to tell us? The enemy might want to capture the DF Station or put it out of commission."

"Boy gum, you moight be roight, Taffy." Gramp cut off a slice of Brown's Mule and popped it into the side of his jaw. He worried the tobacco around until it banked comfortably against his false teeth. "Reckon you and Oi are closer to the ocean than anybody else on this oisland except the service boys. Reckon we got a big job to do. Just keepin' our oyes open and our traps shut. You run along naow and bake them little cakes you been a-frettin' abaout. Don't use more sugar than you have to. It'll be some toime before another ration ticket comes usable. Run on naow and stop askin' me pesky questions."

Taffy busied herself in the small kitchen of the shack. It was Saturday, and she had to clean up the three small rooms where she and Gramp lived. The old man had taught her many things about housekeeping. First, that cleanliness was next to godliness; and second, that she must never waste anything akin to food. She had learned how to wash and iron their clothing and how to mend the tears in Gramp's trousers and her blue jeans. In short, Taffy was as good a housekeeper at thirteen as many grown, married women are at twenty-five.

All during her baking, she kept thinking about

Big Jens and what he had said to Gramp. Her head was so full it was a thousand wonders the little cookies didn't burn to a crisp. But they didn't. Gramp's training about waste caused her to keep a sharp lookout on the old woodstove oven. So the cookies turned out nice and brown, but not burned. Taffy sighed with satisfaction as she viewed the results of her Saturday's baking.

It was hard for her to sit still at supper while Gramp read from the Book. She could hardly keep her attention on the story of Gideon the Mighty. And when Gramp started to say grace, Taffy knew it would be the long one in which he blessed Providence for everything under the sun and the one in which he asked Divine guidance for taking care of her. This was the usual Saturday night ritual. Taffy had been used to it for as long as she could remember. On Sunday morning Gramp always saw to it that she went to Sunday School. That, too, had been a rule.

After the supper dishes were cleared away, Gramp washing and Taffy wiping, they went to Gramp's bedroom and hauled out dark, thick blankets which they nailed over the windows.

"I'll go outside and see if the light shines through," Taffy told him. She walked all around the lean-to and couldn't see a ray. "Reckon I better walk out on the beach a ways just to make sure."

A stiff northeaster was pounding the waves across the beach. Spray hit her in the face as she crossed the first sand fence. She stood on top of a dune and looked toward the shack. All was dark. "Golly, but it's turned cold all of a sudden." She shivered, pulling up the collar of her windbreaker. "Wouldn't be surprised if that old sea does some howling tonight." It was a matter-of-fact thought, with no fear in it. For Taffy was a child of Cape Hatteras, the lonely island off the Graveyard of the Atlantic—Diamond Shoals. She loved the ocean and respected it. But she wasn't afraid of it.

By the time she walked back to the house, Gramp had built a fire in the small tin heater.

"Days are noice and pleasant, but the noights are gettin' roight chilly. You'd best stop goin' barefoot and start wearin' your shoes, Taffy. After all, it's the first of December and winter toime naow."

"Aw, gee, Gramp," Taffy pleaded, "the sand is so nice and warm. I have to wear shoes to school all week. Please let me go barefooted on Saturdays."

"You start wearin' them shoes," Gramp told her firmly. "First thing you know you'll have phthisic pneumony. Oi ain't hankerin' to have no sick youngun on moy hands this winter."

"All right, Gramp, I'll wear them, but I sure do hate it."

"Sounds loike a considerable gale of wind comin' 'cross the dunes. Take the lamp into the bedroom so Oi can open the door and look out. Saounds moighty loike a nor'easter whippin' up."

Taffy did as she was bidden. The oil lamp sputtered as the draft from the door sucked through the cracks of the old shack.

"Whoy, it's cold as blazes aout there," Gramp said, slamming the door, "and it's rainin'. Felt to me loike there was sleet in that rain, too. We're goin' to have a storm. Providence help the seamen on a noight loike this."

The storm grew worse. By three o'clock both Gramp and Taffy rose from their beds and put on their clothes. Gramp built up the fire in the heater, throwing in some dry driftwood.

"Just can't seem to rest durin' a storm," Gramp

said, whittling off a chew of Brown's Mule. Taffy knew why. She knew he was thinking about the storm in which her mother and father were lost at sea.

Just then they heard a sound—a strange, feeble sort of sound, like a cry of distress.

"What was that?" Taffy cried, running to the window and pulling the blanket aside to peer out into the darkness.

"Put that blanket back," Gramp told her sharply. "Don't you remember what Big Jens said abaout that blackaout?"

"I forgot."

The sound came again.

"Get the flashloight," Gramp told her, "and get moy oil clothes and your raincoat."

She ran to do his bidding, excitement lending her speed. The wind slammed the door as they hurried out into the dark, stormy night.

2. Shipwreck

The wind tore over the dunes and the freezing rain stiffened their faces as Taffy and Gramp made their way slowly toward the beach. It was tough going. The northeaster grasped and tugged at them, nearly upending them into the rough, deep sand ruts. Flying sand stung their faces, scraping skin as it went. The night was black as Egypt.

"Oh, I tripped on something," Taffy gasped, pitching headlong into the sand. "What is it?" she called, trying to regain her balance against the wind. "Here's another one of them!"

"Whoy, it's two new automobile tars," Gramp marveled, letting a slim pencil of light hit the ground from his flashlight. Breakers pounded the beach with thunderous fury sending the surf up to their knees. They backed away from the running tide. Then through the frenzied wind they heard the cry.

This time it sounded quite close. "Come on." Gramp gave her a tug. "It's comin' from this direction."

Taffy made another step. Again, she nearly fell. She bent down and felt of the object. Before she could help herself, a strangled scream tore through her throat.

"Shine the light, Gramp," she shrieked. "Look!"

It was a horrible sight that greeted their eyes. There, in the sand, buried up to his neck, was a man! His eyes were open, and in them was such a look of pleading as they had never seen in their lives.

"He's aloive!" Gramp exulted. "Hold the loight whoile Oi troy to dig the sand away."

Taffy stopped sobbing, but her body was shaking as if she had the ague. Stepping on the man's head and feeling his hair when she bent down had completely unnerved her. She laid the flashlight on the ground and quickly rolled enough sand over it so that its beams were severely cut down. "What's he

doing here, Gramp?" she asked through chattering
teeth, helping her grandfather dig the man out of
the sand.

"He must of buried himself to keep from freezin'
to death," Gramp told her. "There's been a shipwreck off the shoals. No tellin' haow many more is
washed up, dead or aloive."

Between the two of them, they managed to drag
the nearly-frozen, half-drowned sailor up to the
shack, where they laid him on Gramp's bunk.

"Wish Oi had a moite of spirits to pour daown
your throat," Gramp worried, as they piled blankets
on the now unconscious man. "Put the coffee pot

on and stir up the far, Taffy. Then go get Big Jens as fast as you can."

Without a bit of fear of the black stormy night, Taffy untied Sailor and jumped on his back. She was still trembling, but there was a job to do. Surefooted and true, the little Banks pony carried her straight to the DF Station. All was dark, but she knew a radio operator was always on duty.

She pounded on a window of the radio control room. It wasn't a second before an armed guard appeared close to her in the darkness. "What goes on here?" he demanded. She felt the cold steel of the pistol he jammed against her arm.

"It's me! Taffy! Gramp says get Big Jens. There's been a shipwreck off the shoals. We just found a half-drowned man buried in the sand. I stepped on his head. And there's automobile tires all over the beach."

"Oh! You sure gave me a turn, Taffy." The guard stuck his gun back into the holster. "I'll get Big Jens out to your place in a jiffy. Get on Sailor and ride home fast. Tell Gramp to watch that man like a hawk. Don't let him get away till the skipper and the boys get there."

"That poor man couldn't go anywhere if he wanted to," Taffy called, mounting the pony. She wheeled Sailor around and went galloping through the screaming northeaster. The little pony sensed Taffy's inner excitement. He took her over the sand fences as if they both had wings. The wind howled through the telephone wires with a savage shriek, sending sheets of icy rain into Taffy's face. Big Jens' station wagon roared by, its lights very dim and low to the ground.

"He'll beat us home, Sailor," she yelled. "Go, boy! Beat that wagon!" But it was no use. The vehicle used by the station as an ambulance was parked in front of the shack when Taffy tied Sailor under the lean-to. "Good boy," she panted, hugging the trembling horse. "You tried, and I'll give you an extra lump of sugar tomorrow."

When she opened the door, Big Jens and three of his crew were standing by the bunk where she and Gramp had laid the man from the beach. He was conscious and trying to sit up. He was talking, but it was the strangest gibberish that Taffy had ever heard.

"What do you make of it, Taylor?" Big Jens was

saying. "He's not talking German. That I know."

"Geek! Geek!" The man gestured wildly and pounded his chest with his hands. "Geek! Geek!"

"Sounds like he's trying to say 'Greek.'" Taffy spoke from the other side of the room.

"By gravy, that's it!" Big Jens exclaimed. "That's exactly it! About nine o'clock last night a Greek ship of Panamanian registry radioed in and asked for a bearing. She reported a high, rough sea and a storm wind. Said she was in no difficulty at the moment. She was carrying . . ." Big Jens turned abruptly to the man on the cot and made circles with his hands. "Was your ship carrying tires? TIRES?" He made more circles with his hands. The man on the cot nodded his head up and down violently. "That ship's foundered on the shoals. Either that or . . ." Big Jens didn't finish. "I can't understand why the station didn't get an SOS."

"Storm probably knocked out their radio," Taylor said.

"There's tars all over the beach aout there," Gramp told them. "Taffy tripped on them."

"Yeah," Big Jens nodded, "and maybe some more men out there too. The life saving crew is on the beach looking. Come on, men, let's get this fellow into the ambulance and over to the sickbay at the station. There's plenty of work to be done before this night's over." Big Jens went over to Taffy and put his arm around her shoulder. "You're a brave girl, Taffy. And Gramp, you're worth every grain of your salt. But remember, not a word of this night's work to anybody." And then he was gone, he and the three crewmen, taking the Greek seaman away with them.

The wind began to die, but the icy rain poured down and the surf pounded on the beach like incessant rolls of thunder. The early hours of the morning were still pitch dark. Gramp shut off the draft on the tin heater. "Moight as well take a chaw of Brown's Mule, Oi reckon. Ain't no more sleep for me this noight. Lay daown, choild," he told Taffy. "Things are in good hands with the coast guard. We done all we could."

"I can't help wondering if there were more men out there," Taffy worried, going to her room to take off her wet clothes.

"Loike as not there was. But they'll foind them. By mornin', the patrol will have scoured every moile of this beach. You get on to bed naow. It's already the

Sabbath. Loike the Book says, 'We pulled our neighbor's ox aout the ditch.' Naow it's toime to rest."

Taffy rolled and tossed, thinking about the shipwreck and the events of the past hours. Suddenly she remembered the strange contraption she had seen on the chimney of the Snyder's old house in the thicket.

"I plum forgot to tell Gramp about it," she said aloud. "Been meaning to all day. Wonder what in tarnation it is? It's higher than the chimney. Come to think about it, it's almost as high as the tower at the DF Station. I'll ask Gramp first thing in the morning." She snuggled under the cover, anticipating the coming of daylight when she could explore the beach. The last thing she heard was the breakers pounding a mad tattoo against the bald sand.

3. Rescue

It was past one o'clock that Sunday, December 7, 1941, before Gramp and Taffy awoke.

"Dagnab old age a-creepin' on me," the old man grumbled, pulling his suspenders over his shoulders. "Naow it's too late for Taffy to get to Sunday School or preachin' either. Ain't got no patience with moyself for oversleepin' on the blessed Sabbath."

"That you, Gramp?" Taffy called sleepily. "Why, the sun's shining. It must be eight o'clock." She came padding from the bedroom in her long nightgown.

"It's eight o'clock all roight," Gramp fussed. "We laid in our bunks till after one o'clock. It's roight down sinful, that's what it is."

"We were awful worn out, Gramp. We had a hard night, remember?"

"Tain't no excuse for sleepin' our loives away." Gramp built a fire of driftwood in the tin heater, and soon the little stove was bouncing up and down with its roaring blaze. "Get your clothes on, choild. Bile me one of them salt mullets for breakfast. Oi'll fix the coffee."

Taffy washed her face in a pan of cold water. Quickly brushing her red-gold hair, she ran to her room and donned clean shirt and jeans. "I'll have something for us to eat in a jiff. My, what a pretty sunshiny day it is! Wouldn't ever think there was such a storm last night."

"That's the old Cape for you," Gramp told her, washing out the coffee pot. "Loike old Stormalong one day, and a paradoise the next. But you listen to them breakers aout there. They still got the saound of storm in them."

"I'm glad we overslept. Now I can go to the beach and look around." Taffy felt so swelled up with excitement she could hardly get the food on the table. But Gramp Morgan attended to her promptly. He wasn't forgetting that it was Sunday.

"You'll listen to the sermon on the radio and learn a passage of Scripture to boot, to remoind you that this is the Lord's Day and meant to be kept holy."

"Oh, Gramp, that will take such a long time. And I'm just perishing to get out on the beach and see what the storm washed up. Please, Gramp."

The old man screwed up his face and looked lovingly at his granddaughter. "Well, we'll wait till supper toime to learn the Scripture. But both of us are goin' to listen to that sermon before we go anywhere. A bit of meditation to reflect on our reckless ways won't hurt neither of us."

Taffy knew it was useless to argue. By the time the dishes were cleared away, it was nearly two o'clock and time to turn on the small battery radio for the Sunday afternoon sermon.

"Gramp, there is the funniest looking thing on the Snyders' chimney. It's some kind of a contraption that looks higher than the tower of Babel. What you reckon it is?" Taffy asked, putting the cups and saucers away.

"Naow, young lady, you ain't been messin' araound that old plantation, have you?" Gramp spoke sternly.

"No, sir. I just saw it yesterday when I went by the old back road to the post office."

"Tain't none of our business. And you and Sailor stay off that back road anyhaow. Reckon if them furriners want to show off to us oislanders, it's their privilege." Gramp snorted. "They don't impress nobody with nothin' exceptin' their unfriendliness. Can't understand whoy some folks are so cantankerous when they get a little wealth poiled up. You stop bein' so curious and keep to the neighborhood trails. Come on naow, and haul up a chair. Sermon'll be over 'fore you know it." He turned on the switch to the radio.

"We interrupt this service for an important announcement," the radio blared. "Japanese bombers operating from carriers have attacked Pearl Harbor Naval Base, its airfields, and barracks. The Japanese planes attacked at dawn. Two of our battleships, a target ship, two destroyers, and a mine layer have been sunk in the attack. This is an emergency."

Gramp and Taffy sat stunned. The radio poured out the treachery of the attack, telling the number of known dead in sailors, soldiers, and civilians, and the tremendous amount of damage done to naval vessels and property.

"Shut it off," Gramp commanded. "Shut it off. The

good Lord preserve us. Naow we'll be in war on two soides of the world. It's plum awful, that's what it is."

"Will war come to us, Gramp? Here? On Cape Hatteras?"

"Oi'm a-thinkin' it's been closer to us than most folks realoized, longer a toime than anybody knew, except maybe the service boys." The old man shook his head worriedly. "All them new men that's been pourin' into the loife savin' stations, all them patrols walkin' the beach with them new-fangled boxes they call walkie-talkies. We've just took too much for granted, choild, thinkin' our help to the British would keep us safe over here. It's a bad toime, Taffy, a bad, bad toime naow."

Taffy felt all choked up and more solemn than she had ever felt in her life. It seemed as if a big claw had reached out from somewhere and was holding her pinned down.

"Ain't nothin' we can do to stop it," Gramp told her. "If and when the toime comes for us to help, then we'll do the best we can. Ain't no need worryin' over trouble. We'll just go on doin' what we've been doin', till we're told otherwoise. Naow Oi'm going to walk over the dunes to Sam Miller's house. Since there ain't goin' to be no sermon, Oi don't care if you go on the beach. But you remember that them waves are heavy with ground swells, so be careful and don't get caught in them."

Taffy promised. But somehow or other the thrill of going to the beach had disappeared. The news on the radio had snuffed out the fun she had planned. Still, it wouldn't do any good to sit in the shack and mope. So she took off toward the ocean.

As she crossed the first sand fence, she spied Lorrie and Malene Scarboro. "Hi. Wait for me," she called, waving to the children. They came running toward her.

"Look at all the tires on the beach down there. The navy's got an armed guard watching them," the children rattled excitedly.

"The Japanese bombed Pearl Harbor today," Taffy told them. "The United States is going to war."

"What did you say?" the girls screeched. "You means the Japs really dropped bombs and blew up Pearl Harbor?"

"That's what the radio said, right at the beginning of the Sunday afternoon sermon."

"Golly, Moses!"

"Malene, you run home and tell Mamma," Lorrie commanded. "She might not have had the radio on." Malene took off down the beach like a frightened rabbit. "Oh, I hope Pop's ship weren't in Pearl Harbor."

Taffy knew that Nat Scarboro, the girls' father, was on a naval vessel somewhere in the Pacific. Nearly all the men on Cape Hatteras were in either the navy or the coast guard. The others who lived there were mostly retired service men or commercial fishermen.

"Can't ever tell where the navy is," Taffy said, worrying the sand around with her foot. "What kind of ship is he on?"

"A tin can—a destroyer."

"Uh huh," Taffy said, turning away, remembering that the radio had said two destroyers had been sunk. She didn't want to tell Lorrie that. "Come on, let's see what's in the surf down there."

"Looks like a big window frame," Lorrie said, running close to the water.

"There's something hanging on it. Look, it's moving," Taffy yelled. The tide was buffeting the piece of debris toward the shore, but the big waves washed it back again as they rolled off the beach. "If I could just get close enough to grab it, maybe you and I could drag it ashore before another wave came."

"I'll wrap one arm around this yaupon tree and hold you with my other," Lorrie told her. "Maybe you can grab it that way. But be careful. The waves are real ploppy today."

Lorrie got a good hold on the yaupon. Taffy flattened herself out on the wet sand. "Hold my leg," she commanded Lorrie. She tried to reach the piece of debris. But a big wave rolled it away. "Slide off a little from the yaupon, Lorrie. That'll give me more reach. I'll get it next time."

The big frame-like object washed in again. There was something alive on it! Taffy grabbed the wreckage. The impact jarred Lorrie loose from the yaupon, sending both girls headlong into a big breaker. The wave landed them on the beach with the force of a rocket, knocking the breath out of them. For a moment they lay still, their hearts pounding so hard their heads were giddy. Shaking off sand and water, they scrambled up before another breaker could pound them into a jelly. They clung to each other, a bit shaken from their experience.

"Look!" Taffy pointed to a shallow pool on the beach about five feet away. There was the piece of wreckage, wallowing its way into the soft sand. Clinging to it and whimpering his heart out was a half-grown puppy!

"Why, he's tied to it," Lorrie exclaimed.

"You poor little thing," Taffy cried, running to the half-drowned pup. "Help me get this rope untied, Lorrie. Wish I had Gramp's knife. The salt water's got these knots soaked hard as rocks."

"Need some help?" A voice spoke near. It was a coast guard patrol.

Lorrie jumped. "Golly, Jess, how you scared me."

"I had my eyes on you kids out there messing in that ocean. Don't you know those waves are too big to monkey with today? It's a thousand wonders you didn't get drowned just now. What you got here? A dog? Well, help me Hanner!" Jess took out his pocket knife and cut the ropes which held the pup to the wooden spar. "Somebody thought a powerful lot of you. Where'd you come from, little feller?" He rubbed the dog's ears.

"Poor little half-drowned pup." Taffy held the dog close to her. "You are beautiful. Must have been on that Greek ship that got wrecked last night," Taffy said before she thought. Jess cut his eyes at her. Lorrie said nothing.

"What you going to do with him?" Jess asked.

Taffy looked at Lorrie with a question in her eyes.

"Oh, he's Taffy's," Lorrie told him. "If I went home with another dog, Mamma would wear my coattails out. We got four beagles already. Pop's rabbit dogs."

"Oh, Lorrie, you sweet thing." Taffy hugged her. "Don't you really want him? Can I really have him?"

"Course you can. I was going to let you have him all the time," Lorrie assured her big-heartedly.

"You kids go home and put on some dry clothes," Jess commanded. "You'll be getting colds, or worse, out here in this cold wind. Go on. Hurry. Besides, I suspect that pup could stand a little drying up, and some warm milk or something to eat." The girls nodded in agreement. Thanking the patrol for his help, they took the puppy and ran over the sand fences back to the shack.

Taffy made up the fire in the tin heater while Lorrie covered the dog with an old blanket.

"Where do you s'pose he came from? A shipwreck,

you reckon?" Lorrie asked, fixing the blanket.

"Must have," Taffy agreed. "But 'finders keepers.' He's my pup now, aren't you, Brandy?"

"What a funny name," Lorrie giggled, helping to hold the pan of warm milk close to the dog's mouth. "Why in tarnation did you name him Brandy?"

"Because he's the color of Miz Sudie's brandywine camphor bottle. That's why. Wonder what kind of dog he is? He's got a face like a bull, but his legs are too long."

"Why he's a boxer, silly," Lorrie told her importantly. "We got two whole books just about dogs. My pop says boxers are about the smartest dogs there are. Reckon your Gramp will let you keep him?"

"Sure he will. He got Sailor for me, didn't he? Gramp likes dogs. Used to have two hounds when I was little. He said they died from old age. I've never had a dog before."

The girls put the puppy behind the stove. He didn't seem to have much life about him. Lorrie dipped her finger in the milk and rubbed it on the dog's mouth. He feebly licked it off.

"Looks like he's about to die," Lorrie said.

"He'll come around all right." Taffy was confident. "I'll get him well if loving and nursing will do it." She added more driftwood to the stove, and soon the old shack was quite warm. "Won't take us long to dry out in here," she told Lorrie. "Take off your boots and put them over Gramp's boot rack. Won't hurt any if we take off our clothes and hang them by the stove. I'll get us some dry ones to put on."

"I'm glad. Mamma would switch me good if I went home wet," Lorrie giggled, as they changed clothes. "She almost didn't let Malene and me come to the beach today anyhow. Got your lessons done for tomorrow?"

"Gee whillikens, no!" Taffy gasped. The excitement of the weekend had made homework pass completely out of her mind.

"Me neither," Lorrie said. "Let's do it. Right now."

"Reckon we'd better," Taffy agreed, "but Gramp will scold if he catches me doing my lessons on Sunday. He says Bible lessons are all a person ought to do on Sunday."

"Your Gramp is a funny old cudgermudgeon, isn't he?" Lorrie laughed.

"That's not so, Lorrie Scarboro," Taffy turned on

her friend. "He's the dearest Gramp in the world. And don't you be calling him names, either."

"Oh, shucks, I didn't mean anything," Lorrie apologized.

"You'd better not," Taffy told her sternly. "Now let's see. We got to do arithmetic. I just hate those old decimals, don't you? I always get that little dot in the wrong place."

The girls worked busily at their figures, Taffy keeping an eye on the pup behind the stove. He seemed to be sleeping. It wasn't long before their arithmetic was finished.

"We've got current events tomorrow," Lorrie remembered. "Every Monday, just as regular as clockwork, the last fifteen minutes of history lesson. I wish Miss White would forget about it sometime. But she's got a memory like an elephant."

"Well, something big happened in the world today," Taffy told her solemnly. "Guess none of us will have trouble giving current events tomorrow."

"Yeah," Lorrie answered seriously. "Wish I knew where Pop's ship was today. Reckon I need to get home. Mamma will be worried about me and about Pop too. Did the radio say anything about any tin cans getting sunk when the Japs bombed Pearl Harbor?"

Taffy put her pencil to her lips and mumbled something about how aggravating it was to unscramble the parts of speech in a sentence. "Wonder if I'll ever talk with proper grammar? Miss White says my speech is a caution to hear."

"Mine too," Lorrie giggled. "Teacher calls it our Elizabethan brogue. Whatever that means!"

"Oh, I'll learn to talk proper. I'm going to study to be a teacher like Miss White when I go to college." Taffy took a long breath, glad that the subject of destroyers was safely over. She didn't want to be the one to tell Lorrie that two of them had been sunk by Jap bombs that morning. Down in the pit of her stomach she had a sinky feeling that Lorrie's Pop might have been on one of those vessels.

"Say, Taffy, have you seen that funny-looking thing on the Snyders' chimney?" Lorrie asked her. "Gosh all hemlock, it's high as a Georgia pine!"

"Yes, sure is," Taffy agreed. "I saw it yesterday when I went to the post office. What you suppose it is? Gramp says he thinks it's just something else they want to show off to the islanders."

"Yeah, reckon so. They are funny folks, them Yankees. Ben Oden and John Gaskins were walking home from Trent one night about two weeks ago. When they passed through the thicket they heard all kinds of hammering and sawing coming from the Snyder place. It was late, too. About one o'clock."

"Bet they were nailing it up right then," Taffy nodded her head.

"Night's a funny time to be putting things up. Mom said the young Snyder drove by our house in his pickup truck just before sundown that day. He had lots of big crates piled up in the truck. Mom said she reckoned he'd just come in on the four-o'clock ferry. Next day we kids rode our horses down through the thicket. There wasn't any sign of life around the place. Quiet as the grave. It was then we saw that funny looking contraption set up against the chimney. You could hardly tell it was there because it blended right in with the pine trees."

"I can't imagine what the Snyders are up to. Don't any of the islanders ever go there. Gramp went to the gate once and sold some mullets. One of the Snyder boys took them. Didn't ask Gramp in, either. Funny folks, I call them."

"You can say that again. It's queer none of the she Snyders have been down here since that first summer they bought the place. Reckon they feel too hifaluting to mingle with the rest of us," Lorrie sniffed. "I hear they live in a fancy house up in Baltimore, and the children go to some kind of a funnynamed school—pinnochial, or something like that. Old lady Snyder told Miz Oden one day when she was at the post office."

Taffy giggled. "Whoever heard of such?"

"My, but today has been exciting. We got a new dog, and our homework's all done. I got to go before Mamma comes hunting me with the razor strap. I'll see you in school tomorrow." Lorrie quickly changed clothes and peeked at the puppy. The sun was sinking behind the dunes when she waved goodby.

Taffy busied herself fixing supper. She stirred up the fire and added more driftwood. The pup whined and stirred in his sleep.

"Just let me fix the blankets over the windows and light the lamp, Brandy. Then I'll give you some more warm milk."

Gramp stepped up on the stoop at the back door. Taffy greeted him with happiness shining in her face.

"Come see my new pup, Gramp. Me and Lorrie got him right out of the ocean."

"Naow can you beat that?" the old man marveled, pulling the blanket aside. "And he's sure enough as pretty a pup as Oi ever saw." He rubbed the dog's ears. "Baout done in too, ain't you, little feller?"

"I gave him some milk, Gramp. Hope you don't mind."

"Certainly not," Gramp told her emphatically. "The good Lord knows even when a sparrow falls. Reckon it behooves us humans to do what we can for animals in distress. Soides, he's a foine dog. He'll grow up to be a good one, too. Oi don't reckon we'll be any worse off for givin' him a few cans of milk. Come on naow, let's eat our supper and get these dishes cleared away. We both need to get some sleep. Tomorrow is Monday. You got to roise early and get ready for school. Got your lessons done?"

"Yes, sir," she nodded, feeling guilty for having just finished them on the Sabbath.

Gramp said the grace and they ate. All during the meal the old man was in a deep study. He didn't talk about his fishing plans for the coming week as he usually did. Taffy noticed it.

"Did you have a nice visit at Sam Miller's house, Gramp?"

"Yep," Gramp nodded. "Lots of old-toimers was over there chewin' the fat. Everybody's tongue was a-waggin' abaout the Japs bummin' Pearl Harbor."

"Did anybody mention that thing on the Snyders' roof?"

Gramp looked up sharply from his plate. "Funny you asked that. Come to think abaout it, somebody did mention it, but Oi disremember who it was. Come on, let's get the table cleared away."

Taffy sighed and got up. She knew there wasn't any use in trying to find out what was on Gramp's mind if he didn't want to tell her. "Sometimes it's plain discouraging," she thought to herself. "Reckon my curiosity will get me in Dutch one of these days, but I sure would like to know what's worrying Gramp."

Long after Taffy had fallen into a troubled sleep, Gramp still lay awake. He wasn't particularly worried about the things he had heard over at Sam Miller's house. But he was curious. Seemed as if everybody over there was steamed up about the comings and goings of the Snyders. Pam Gaskins hinted that something queer was in the wind. John Hawkins even came right out and said he believed the Snyders were making moonshine whiskey and selling it on the mainland. Said he believed that thing on the chimney was a part of the still they used to make the whiskey. Gramp had listened, keeping his thoughts to himself. The young Snyder who had bought the mullets at the gate that morning was perfectly capable of being a moonshiner or a highway robber either, Gramp thought to himself. "Toime'll tell," he yawned, pulling the blanket up over his old bones. "Oi just hope Taffy don't get too curious. That youngun's a soight, the way she asks questions abaout things. Reckon that new pup will keep her aout of mischief for a whoile though," he said, as he scrooched down under the cover.

Taffy rolled and tossed in her sleep, dreaming of flying monsters with bombs strapped to their tails.

4. Ash Cans
and Broken Glass

Excitement ran rampant in the island school on Monday. Taffy had never seen a day that flew by so fast. Miss White changed the whole order of the usual morning schedule so that they could talk about the bombing of Pearl Harbor. Hands kept waving in the air, and questions poured from the children's lips. Billie Evans wanted to know what would happen on the island now.

"Let's review what's been happening," Miss White answered. "If you will think back, you will discover lots of ways we've already been affected, even though we haven't been in a state of war."

"Yeah," Tommie Oden interrupted, "the Battle of the Atlantic between German subs and British ships."

"That's right," continued Miss White, "because Great Britain has had to keep her sea routes open to the United States so she can get supplies."

"Boy," Glen Gaskins said, round-eyed, "now we'll be fighting alongside the British."

The teacher nodded. "And it's going to be more and more dangerous to convoy men and materiel across the ocean."

"All them big tankers going by the Cape," Billie gulped. "Pop says they're loaded with oil and gasoline for the British."

"Won't surprise me if those tankers draw submarines like flies," Lorrie added solemnly. Taffy nodded her head in agreement.

"Submarines are very different from what they were in World War I," Miss White told them. "Now they can go great distances. But, children, we must not get so excited about all this that we can't carry on our day-to-day activities. We have to be alert, but we all have our own jobs to do. Just as always." The children nodded. One reason they liked Miss

White so well was that she never tried to fool them about anything. She just talked about things man to man and made them feel proud to be a part of everything. "And, children," she went on, "you know that loose talk and gossip help the enemy. Many of your fathers and brothers are in some branch of the armed services. Many of them are on ships. So guard your tongues. Don't answer questions that strangers might ask about them."

Again the children nodded in silent agreement. They fully understood the teacher. It was true. Their kinfolk were in the services. Some of them were helping to man the oil tankers of the maritime service as well as the big cargo ships that carried war materials to Europe. Then, too, didn't they live on an island beach where government installations were strung all up and down the coast? They knew the importance of keeping silent tongues in their heads.

Taffy was thoughtful as she rode Sailor home from school. She couldn't help wondering if Nat Scarboro's ship had been one of the destroyers sunk at Pearl Harbor. She still had that empty feeling about it. It might be weeks or even months before they heard.

December sped. Christmas came and went without the usual festive events that took place on the
island. The Old Christmas celebration at Rodanthe
was canceled. Old Buck, the apparition from Trent
woods who made his appearance each Old Christmas, stayed deep within the vastness of the forest.
Taffy missed the usual oyster roast and program at
the school. But she understood why they could not
be held. Gramp gave her a beautiful collar for
Brandy as a Christmas gift. The pup had completely
survived his shipwreck and followed Taffy everywhere, trotting contentedly at Sailor's heels when
she rode the pony. He had even followed her to
school. But Gramp put his foot down about that.

"Sailor's enough to go to school," he told Taffy.
"Soides, you know very well the teacher ain't hankerin' to have no dogs layin' up in her classroom.
And what if he wandered off somewhere. Brandy'll
stay roight home with me." To tell the truth, Gramp
loved the dog almost as much as Taffy did. When he
went fishing in the afternoon, Brandy sat in the bow
of the skiff. Gramp had taught him not to bark when
he pulled in a net of shiny fish. He had taught him
to be quiet when he sighted a school of mullets

swimming close to the bow of the boat. He had also taught the dog to retrieve. Brandy was an apt pupil. He grew like a weed. In two months he looked like a grown dog.

War wrought changes on the island. Gasoline became rationed, as were tires and many other commodities. Canned milk was put on the ration list. Even the quinine which Gramp took for the ague was now rationed. The Japanese had captured the islands of the south Pacific where tin and quinine were produced, thus cutting off the world supply. Commercial fishermen and all others who had boats of a certain size were required to register with the coast guard. Even the pleasure yachts anchored off Hatteras Inlet were taken over by the government for patrol duty. New sickbays (government infirmaries) were built at Nags Head, Cape Hatteras, and Ocracoke. The coast guard station at Ocracoke was converted into a naval base. Secret installations were put in at the Pea Island Life Saving Station, and top secret apparatus was brought to the DF Station. The beaches were crawling with jeeps manned by stern-looking sailors who were armed to the teeth and who wore the queer boxes called walkie-talkies strapped to their bodies.

Taffy watched a construction gang build a tall tower not five hundred yards from Gramp's shack. The area around it was restricted, and Big Jens gave strict orders to stay away from it.

"It's super-secret stuff, Taffy," he told her. "No civilians even suspect what it's going to be. But you can just bet it's something that will help make our coast a safer place." Taffy listened and obeyed.

Even the old candy-stick lighthouse became restricted. It was to be used as a lookout post. The steel skeleton tower over in Buxton woods still sent out its long rays of light over the ocean, warning mariners of the shifting sands of nearby Diamond Shoals.

At school, the children got in little bunches at recess times and whispered about things.

"They got a submarine off Cape Henry last week," Malene told Taffy in the washroom.

"Oh, my mercy," she gasped. "Why, Cape Henry's real close. How do you know? Who told you?"

"I can't tell. But it's so. And I know the navy and coast guard are expecting subs off our own beach too," she whispered. "You and Gramp better be careful out there in that shack or you might get torpedoed some night." She giggled nervously.

"Silly goose. What would a submarine want to waste a torpedo on our old shack for?"

"That new tower, you nut. You see those patrol boats out there every day, don't you? What do you think they're looking for? Bluefish? Well, not much they ain't."

"Golly, Moses." Taffy shivered. "I never even thought of that. Do you reckon they're really hunting U-boats?"

"Course they are. The whole ocean is full of subs. Didn't Miss White tell us about how hard it was going to be to get supplies across the ocean? The Nazi U-boats are probably just lying in wait for every convoy sailing out there."

The bell rang. The afternoon recess was over.

"Now, children, we must start thinking about our club meeting for next week," Miss White began when the room had settled down. "Taffy, you and Albert can collect the . . ."

BOOM! BOOM!

Whatever the teacher was about to say was cut off by the crashing of glass which fell into the schoolroom from the windows.

BOOM! BOOM! More glass. The schoolhouse shook and seemed to rock on its foundations. For seconds, both children and teacher sat mute in stunned surprise. Then they scrambled under their desks like scared rabbits.

"Something is being bombed!" Mel Quidley yelled. "And it's not the schoolhouse. It's on the beach! And I'm going to see what it is!" He streaked out of the classroom like a bolt of lightning.

"Mel, you come back here," Miss White commanded. But she might as well have saved her breath. Taffy was the next one to bolt. Then there was a wholesale exodus from the seventh-grade room. Crashing explosions continued to shake the building. "I'll not be left here in an empty room," Miss White gasped, crawling from under her desk. And off she took after the children in the direction of the beach. In less than five minutes she was there and had gathered her little group together. Armed guards held them a good way back from the surf.

About six miles off shore, patrol boats were circling madly. At close intervals the boats dropped depth charges into the ocean. Moments later there were terrific explosions, with water flying forty feet into the air.

"Lookie, there comes a coast guard cutter," Belton yelled. "Boy, oh boy, now you'll really see some action."

"Children, we must get back," the teacher said sternly.

"Oh, teacher, please," the children clustered around begging.

"It's too dangerous," Miss White told them. "We have no business being out here."

"You're right, ma'am," the guard told her. "But these island kids are as fearless as they come. Since they are already here, you might as well let them stay and see what happens to an enemy sub when Uncle Sam's Navy goes into action." He grinned.

"Oh," the teacher gasped. "Well, for just a moment then. I'm sure we wouldn't get any lessons done now."

"I'm not hankering for any more glass to clip me

on the back of the neck, either," Belton grinned.

"Why, you did get cut." Miss White was all concern. "Here, let me see." Sure enough Belton's neck was cut and bleeding. The teacher wiped off the blood and tied her handkerchief around his neck.

"Shucks, 'tain't nothin'." Belton blushed at all the attention. He wasn't used to being a hero.

"Want to see through these binoculars, ma'am?" the guard said. "Looks like the cutter's going to unload some ash cans." The guard passed the glasses to the teacher.

"Let us see," the children begged. So one by one the youngsters were allowed to look. The explosions offshore were deafening. Taffy held her ears. She was dying to get down closer to the beach. But she knew she'd better not try it in face of the teacher and the guard's orders.

An explosion, greater than the others, hit the air. Water flew mountain high. Then the patrol boats and cutter started sailing rapidly south toward Hatteras Inlet.

"Where they going?" Taffy wanted to know.

"Not far," the guard told her. "Guess you'd all better get back now. Stay off the beach and remember to keep quiet about this afternoon. Anything you say might help the enemy." Then he was **gone** down to the water's edge to join the other armed guards.

"It's nearly three-thirty, children," Miss White said. "When we get back, it will be time to dismiss and go home. Whatever will our principal say?"

"Don't worry about that, teacher," Bob Mallison told her. "Look down yonder and you'll see the rest of the younguns and the principal just turning back toward the school. They came out too."

Back at the schoolhouse, Taffy lost no time untying Sailor and making off toward home. She cut across John Gaskill's field, Sailor taking the rail fence easy as pie. The route offered a short cut to the beach. She hoped and prayed the armed guards would be gone by the time she got there. Topping a dune inside the fence, she strained her eyes against the evening sun and looked up and down the beach. There was only one jeep in sight, and it was down on the end of the Cape. Her conscience chided her for her disobedience, but her curiosity was stronger at the moment.

"Go, boy. Down to the surf," she directed the

pony. Sailor loped along in an easy canter. The waves were washing in and leaving a black, gooey substance on the beach. The horse snorted and shied to the right, away from the stuff.

"Wonder what it is?" Taffy stopped the pony and got down. "Why, it smells like oil." She mounted again and slowly walked the horse down the beach opposite the place where the patrol boats and cutter had dropped depth charges earlier in the afternoon. The pony shied again, snorting viciously. "What's the matter, boy?" Taffy looked down on the sand. There in her path was a loon. "Whoa, Sailor." Again she dismounted. She looked at the helpless bird. "You poor thing, you can't fly. And no wonder. Your wings are all full of that mess of goo."

Sure enough, the bird's wings were so soaked with the stuff that he couldn't take off. He flopped all over the sand. The beach as far as Taffy's eyes could reach was beginning to have the same black slime on it. On her way home, she saw a dozen more loons with gooed-up feathers. Taffy felt sorry, but mostly she was mad. When even the poor animals had to suffer because of the enemy, that was too much! She was muttering to herself angrily when Big Jens stopped her just as she turned on the path toward home.

"Well, I reckon you saw it all, young lady?" he grinned. "From the first ash can to the last one? Notice all that oil slick washing up?"

"So it is oil," Taffy said. "Where'd it come from?"

"Could be from a torpedoed British tanker. But I like to think it came right out of the middle of one of Adolph's submarines," he told her. "Reckon he's short one Nazi U-boat this day."

"It was horrible." Taffy shuddered, thinking of the men who might have gone down in the sub.

"War is horrible, Taffy. You kids here on the Cape are living pretty close to it nowadays, too. Well, there's no help for it. This is your home."

"Big Jens, why are depth charges called 'ash cans'?"

"Oh, that? Well, it's because the explosives are packed in containers that look something like garbage tins. Guess some sailor nicknamed them that. Why do you ask?"

"No reason, except we've been talking about things in our current events class at school. Teacher says they are depth charges and that we shouldn't use slang like 'tin cans' for destroyers and 'ash cans' for depth charges."

Big Jens laughed. "That's the penalty for having a 'furriner' as a teacher. First thing you know she'll have you kids talking so proper I won't be able to understand you."

"Shucks, I won't," Taffy grinned. "Big Jens," she began hesitatingly, "what's that strange contraption up there on the Snyders' chimney? Have you noticed it?"

The chief of the DF Station looked up at the girl sharply. "Yeah, come to think about it, I did notice it, Taffy." Big Jens was worried about Taffy's curiosity, but he couldn't let on. "Guess the Snyders aim to do some roof repair or clean out their chimney," he told her nonchalantly.

"Nobody ever seems to be at home," Taffy went on. "Windows are all boarded up. I heard Nike Lewis, the storekeeper, say they haven't bought any groceries in a long time. But they must come and go, because Malene's mamma saw their truck go by the other day all loaded with crates and big boxes."

"I'd say they were right unfriendly folks to be living in such a friendly village," Big Jens told her.

"Yeah," Taffy agreed. "But I surely would like to take one peep inside that house. Bet they got it fixed up like a New York mansion." She sighed.

"Shucks, Taffy, you and Gramp have got more happiness wrapped up in your little shack than all

the mansions in the world. I wouldn't worry any about that old house on the knoll. Better get home or your grandfather will wonder what has become of you. You and Gramp keep a sharp eye," the skipper admonished. "Things are getting a bit lively down here on the Cape."

5. Torpedo Junction

Big Jens could never have been more correct. Things did get plenty lively—from submarine warfare! In two months the ocean off the shores of Cape Hatteras became known as Torpedo Junction!

The island folk listened to booming explosions both night and day as tankers met their doom from German U-boats. Gramp and Taffy went about their tasks the same as usual, except that Taffy did not ride on the beach as often as before. She was strictly forbidden to go there after dark.

Taffy had just fed Sailor his evening oats and carried in an armful of driftwood that evening in January. Gramp was trimming the wick in the oil lamp. Just as Taffy threw down the wood, three deafening explosions boomed across the water; and then three more. The little shack rocked; the windows rattled. Taffy's eardrums felt blasted.

They quickly opened the door and went outside. Up the beach, off Rodanthe or Gull Shoal—somewhere in that vicinity—two tremendous fires were blazing over the ocean. They seemed to be about ten miles offshore. Another explosion smote their ears, sending up a bigger blaze near the first two.

"How awful!" Taffy shuddered clutching her grandfather's hand.

"Subs hittin' a convoy," Gramp told her. "Tankers loaded with oil. That's what it is."

"But sinking three ships at a time," Taffy whimpered. "It's horrible!"

"Yes, child," Gramp tried to comfort her, "war always is. But think of them little children over in Europe, and all the sufferin' in the Pacific oislands."

"But the subs come so close to shore, Gramp. Isn't there anything our ships can do to protect themselves?"

They walked back to the shack. "It's a bad toime, roight now," Gramp told her. "The truth of the

matter is, we was caught in an awful state of unpre-
paredness, what with them Japs bummin' us at Pearl
Harbor and us a-troyin' to help the British keep the
sea lanes open 'twixt here and Europe. It'll take
toime, but don't you fret. Our country won't take all
this loyin' down. You mark moy words."

"But think of all those poor sailors out there in
that blazing sea," Taffy cried, tears sliding off her
nose.

"Yep. There's danger a-plenty what with burnin'
to death, drownin', and the fear of havin' their loife
boats pulled into the goiant propellers of them big
ships. Hand me that skein of twoine. You can hold
it on your arms whoile Oi ball it up. Got a lot of net
mendin' to do tomorrow."

"Wonder how many subs are out there?" Taffy
asked, moving her arms in rhythm as her grandfather
balled the twine. "Do they have to go all the way
back to Germany to get refueled?"

Gramp Morgan sighed, realizing he hadn't been
able to take Taffy's mind off the sinkings. "Well,
there ain't no tellin'," he answered. "Moight be as
many as twenty operatin' in the Atlantic. Probably
them foive-hundred-ton craft too, with four torpedo

tubes for'ard and one a-stern. They carry anywhere from twelve to fourteen torpedoes, besoides their deck guns. Reckon they can run six weeks or more on the amaount of fuel they carry."

"Listen to the jeeps and trucks going up the beach." Taffy turned her head. "Bet the lifesaving stations will be busy this night."

"Lots of airplanes goin' over too. The DF Station boys must've radioed the Norfolk Navy Base to send daown planes to hunt the subs."

That was the middle of January, 1942. By the end of the month nearly a dozen ships had been sent to the bottom. In February nearly a dozen more were sunk off the coast. Freighters, cargo vessels, oil tankers, passenger liners—all went down as they attempted to make the dash around Cape Hatteras. By March, the submarines were cruising in packs instead of singly. It became common knowledge that two or three U-boats were plying the waters off Diamond Shoals.

One day when Big Jens came for fish, Taffy heard him say to Gramp:

"Yes, sir, Gramp Morgan, just as sure as I'm a Scandihoovian, I believe there's a mother submarine anchored off there somewhere. She rests on the sandy bottom all day just lying in wait. At night she comes up to charge her batteries. Probably she's supplying several baby subs. Maybe that's why so many ships get sunk. So far they've been too smart for our planes to spot them."

Gramp Morgan shook his head and worried.

In the middle of March, the U-boats had a field day. Islanders talked in subdued tones about the sinking of three tankers and two freighters in the space of twenty-four hours. Taffy listened to their talk when she went to the village store. "They say the ocean was a blazin' inferno from here to Cape Lookaout," Nike was saying, as he weighed out rationed sugar. "They attacked the convoy roight and left."

By the end of the month, it was said that the subs had sunk an average of almost a ship a day off the North Carolina coast. But life went on. The islanders went about their work as usual, perhaps a little more grimly.

April came, bringing a breath of summer to Cape Hatteras. It was on a Saturday that Big Jens and his son Kenny came riding up to the shack in the station jeep. Gramp had caught a big channel bass in his net, and Big Jens had come to get it. Gramp and the islanders called the big channel bass "old drums." This one would weigh thirty pounds or more.

"My crew will really go for some baked channel bass," the skipper told Gramp. "The station cook knows how to wrastle up a pretty good tangy sauce too."

"Well, he's a noice fish," Gramp told him, pocketing the dollar bill which the chief gave him.

Kenny Jens was about a year older than Taffy and a head taller. The perpetual grin on his freckled face was as genuine as his friendship with the island youngsters. This was obvious, as he and Taffy raced Brandy down the beach until they fell laughing and panting on the sand.

"Make out like you're going to hit me, Kenny," Taffy said, "and see what Brandy does."

Kenny jumped up and came at Taffy with his fist drawn back. The dog growled viciously and sailed on Kenny, knocking the surprised boy to the ground. He held him fast by the arm, his teeth not quite sinking through his sleeve, as he stood over Kenny, nailing him to the ground. You could tell the dog meant business.

"Hey, call him off. I wasn't going to hurt you," Kenny yelled half in fear and half in anger at being caught by surprise.

"Turn him loose, Brandy," Taffy commanded. The dog trotted over to her, looking up for approval. Taffy grinned as she rubbed Brandy's ears.

"Who taught him to do that?" Kenny blustered, brushing the sand off his clothes. "Why, gee whillikins, he's as smart as the trained service dogs."

"It's a secret. I can't tell you. Even Gramp doesn't know about it," Taffy assured him.

"Well, it's a smart trick all right. Bet I don't ever try that any more." He grinned shyly. "Say, I'll tell you a secret if you'll tell me who taught Brandy."

"I don't know if I should." Taffy hesitated, reluctant to give away a confidence. "Do you honestly declare you won't ever tell a living soul?"

"Course I won't tell, you dope. You'd better not spill to anybody what I tell you, either. Because if Pop found out, he'd whale the daylights out of me."

"Well," Taffy looked around to make sure Gramp

and Big Jens were out of hearing. "You know Joe Hanes, that fellow who handles the dogs that the patrols use at night?"

"Yeah. He's got quarters at the station with the DF crew."

"Well, one day he saw Brandy and me out on the beach. He made friends with Brandy right away. Said a boxer was a smart dog and could be trained real easy. Lots of evenings after school Brandy and I have slipped out on the beach when Joe's been on patrol. Joe taught him that trick and lots of others too. Said they might come in handy sometime. Course he doesn't want anybody to know. Said the chief would be awful mad."

"My Pop's the chief," Kenny laughed, "and I bet he'd dress Joe down good fashion if he knew. But what Pop don't know won't hurt him." Taffy giggled. "Now let me tell you something," Kenny went on. "You remember hearing the explosions offshore night before last?" Taffy nodded. "Well, sir, guess what? A passenger ship on its way to New York from Capetown, Africa, was torpedoed. I overheard one of the radio operators tell another one just as they were changing the watches at eight o'clock. He said it real low, but I heard every word. And that isn't all I heard, either," he told Taffy, pausing dramatically.

"What else?" Taffy asked, hanging breathlessly on every word.

"A baby was born right there on the ocean in a life boat."

"Gee whillikins!" Taffy gasped.

"And guess what? A destroyer picked them up from the life boat—mother, doctor, baby, and all! And they named the baby after the destroyer!"

"Boy, you sure got an earful," the girl told him admiringly.

"I'll tell you something else, too," Kenny came closer and whispered. "Some of us boys crept down through that thicket of pines on the back road one night about a week ago, and guess what we saw?"

"What?" Taffy asked excitedly.

"We saw a light shining through the cracks of the boarded windows of the Snyder house. Nobody's supposed to be there, either. Old man Snyder and his son left over two weeks ago. Pop saw them going on the Oregon Inlet ferry the day he went up to the base in Norfolk.

"Who you reckon it was?" Taffy whispered back. "Think somebody broke into their house while they were gone?"

"I got other ideas. But I'm not talking. Have you seen that funny thing on the roof over there?"

"I sure have. Looks like some kind of machine they might use to clean out the chimney."

"Huh," Kenny snorted, "I expect it's for sweeping other things besides chimneys. But don't you dare tell anybody. Pop would skin me alive if he knew I had been out that late at night. I was scared stiff that the man on duty at the station was going to catch me crawling back into my window. Now promise you won't say a word."

"Of course I won't, Kenny."

"KENNY! TAFFY!" Big Jens bellowed. "You kids come over here."

The youngsters went running back to the shack, Brandy at their heels.

"Pile into the jeep," the chief said. "One of the patrols told me that a big whale just washed up on the beach between here and Hatteras Inlet. Thought you kids might like to see him."

"Wowie," Taffy hollered. "You bet!"

The skipper stowed his fish in a tarpaulin in the back of the jeep. "Come on, Gramp, you can ride up here with me. Let the kids pile in with the fish."

"Can't say this contraption is much for comfort," Gramp groaned, as the jeep made its rough way through the serpentine sand tracks.

"Nope, it isn't a Rolls-Royce, Gramp," Big Jens grinned. "But she'll take us through this deep sand without getting stuck. Wonderful thing, this four-wheel drive."

In fifteen minutes they arrived where the huge whale was lying on the beach.

"Jiminy, but he's a big one," Gramp exclaimed. "Can't say that Oi've ever seen a bigger one in moy whole loife."

"What happened to him?" Taffy wanted to know.

"Shucks, that's easy," Kenny told her importantly. "Some of our patrol boats saw him gliding under the water, thought he was a sub, and dumped an ash can on him."

"He'd be blowed to pieces, if that happened," Gramp told him.

"Well, maybe they didn't make a direct hit. Maybe the shock killed him."

"Now, you know, Gramp, that could have been just what did happen," Big Jens added. "It would be easy to mistake a big whale for a sub. Particularly at night."

"See?" Kenny grinned.

"Will anyone come down and cut up the whale for the oil?" Taffy asked.

"We'll notify the folks that used to do it," Big Jens told her. "But I doubt seriously whether anyone will, now that it's wartime."

"He sure is big," Taffy said, walking down to the mammoth head.

"Reckon one loike that could swallow Jonah all roight," Gramp commented.

"Well, pile back in. I've got to get back to the station. It's nearly sundown," Big Jens told them.

"Hope it's quoiet in these parts tonoight," Gramp said, as he and Taffy crawled out of the jeep.

"There's no promise of it," the chief replied worriedly. "Nope, there's no promise of it."

"I hear tell that them U-boats has sunk fifty or more ships off our North Caroloiner coasts these last noinety days," Gramp told him.

"Gramp Morgan, you never cease to amaze me.

You must have second sight or something. For a man who tends his own business as well as you do, how do you find out so much?"

"Oi got good ears," Gramp snorted, "and there ain't nothin' wrong with moy oyesoight neither."

Big Jens shook his head wonderingly as he and Kenny took off toward the station.

By mid-April all the coastal villages were placed under a strict blackout, even though some of them were a good way from the ocean. The community stores did a land-office business selling a new commodity—black window curtains. Gramp gave Taffy money to buy four shades to replace the blankets which they had kept nailed to the windows.

"Wonder why the villages away from the beach have to be blacked out?" Taffy asked George Miller, the storekeeper, while she was making her purchases.

"Well, Oi don't roightly know, Taffy," George told her. "Oi heard that the submarines always surface at noight beyond the shippin' lanes. Guess they can see the convoys and tankers silhouetted against the loights on the shore. Up till naow our ships have just been sittin' ducks for the U-boats."

"Oi heard tell," Ben Gaskins spoke up, "that even the weather reports are goin' to be blacked aout."

"Censored, Ben, not blacked aout," George corrected him.

"Well, it's all the same. A body won't even know from naow on what koind of fishin' weather to expect. Looks loike our goverment could do somethin' to get shet of them U-boats," Ben complained.

"Oi'm surproised at you, Ben," George chided. "That koind of talk is just what the enemy wants. Don't you fret. Uncle Sam may be slow, but he's sure. You mark moy words, you ain't goin' to hear of so many sinkin's from naow on."

Taffy paid for her purchases and made her way out of the store. She was very thoughtful as she mounted Sailor and started home. She wondered what George had meant. The sun was setting as she crossed the sand fence in front of the shack. In thirty minutes she and Gramp had fixed the blackout shades at the windows.

"First curtains ever been put to them windows," Gramp told her. "Ain't never needed none before."

"I think they look pretty," Taffy said, proud of their new possessions.

"The reason they're up there ain't so pretty," Gramp told her soberly. "Black draperies . . ." he started, but decided not to finish his statement.

Taffy nodded, knowing what he was going to say. She thought of the torpedoed ships she had watched burning on the dark stretches of the ocean. Her heart felt heavy. She wondered how much longer the destruction to shipping would last. Each night she said a prayer that the war would end.

But April slid into May, and ships were still being sunk off the coast. More and more patrol boats could be seen plying the waters off Diamond Shoals. British armed trawlers joined American patrols and aircraft in their ceaseless task of tracking down U-boats. Often, word of "a kill" would drift into the gossip of the village. Cape Lookout was made into a protected anchorage. The distance to safety was now shorter, and ships could proceed at night blacked out against the enemy. But Nazi submarines still plied their persistent, deadly trade off the North Carolina coast.

6. Saboteur!

School let out on the island. Taffy and her friends spent their days on the Sound shore, since the ocean beach had become restricted in so many places. They crabbed the shallow sand bars in Pamlico Sound and picked the wild dewberries that grew on the shore.

Brandy grew into his full size and was Taffy's shadow. Many of the service boys wanted to buy him.

"I'll give you fifty dollars for him," Joe Ellis told her one day.

"No, sir, not for fifty hundred," Taffy affirmed. I fished him out of the ocean when he was a pup. I just couldn't stand to part with him."

"He's a purebred boxer all right," Joe said,

scratching the dog's ears. "Wonder where he came from?"

"That I can't say. He was tied to a spar. Guess his owner wanted to make sure he washed ashore. Poor pup, he was nearly gone when I got him." She hugged the big dog as if he were a human.

May passed into the first hot days of June. Taffy and the Scarboro girls gathered blackberries off the sand fences and sold them to the villagers. They roamed the woods, getting branches of yellow jessamine and climax. But the shadow of worry was ever present over them. Their summer happiness was not as real as it had been in former years.

Conflict raged bitterly on both sides of the world. Many of the island folk received telegrams from the services telling them of sons, brothers, sweethearts, or fathers being lost in Pacific naval battles or on the European continent. Taffy's heart was gladdened when Malene told her that her father had not been in Pearl Harbor that fateful Sunday. But sadness and gloom plagued the people of the island.

Sam Mills' boy was lost in the Battle of Midway. Late in June, a coast guard truck brought in a flag-draped, metallic coffin containing the mortal remains of Ben Daniels' youngest son, Hal. The boy had lost his life in a patrol craft badly damaged in the Atlantic. Taffy and Gramp went to the funeral. All the village folks turned out. It was their way of showing the bereaved family the high esteem they had for Hal and his service to his country.

The military funeral was the first that Taffy had ever witnessed. She watched the grim-faced honor guard standing at attention beside the grave. Five of them. They stood straight and tall in their full-navy uniforms, their guns held stiffly against their shoulders. Then came the place in the ritual where their leader gave the order to fire. In rapid succession, three volleys sounded over the grave. Off in the distance, the sound of "Taps" could be heard, played by a bugler who was not in sight. A big lump came into Taffy's throat.

Taffy and Gramp walked home from the cemetery in the still summer air. They shared in their hearts the heavy sadness of all their neighbors who had kinfolk in the various theaters of war. The threat of the submarines hiding out in the ocean off their shores added fear and sorrow.

As summer wore on, they heard whisperings of

more dreadful things. Saboteurs! Spies who appeared out of nowhere and set fires, wrecked trains,
blew up railroads!

Gramp's wrinkled old face set into stern lines. He
got out Old Betsy—his muzzle loader—oiled the gun,
and worked over it until it was in perfect order. He
became stricter about Taffy's comings and goings,
always cautioning her to stay off the beach. He gave
specific orders for her not to ride Sailor on the back
road by the boarded-up house in the thicket. He
didn't like the talk he heard in the village about the
strange doings around that place. He knew Taffy's
curiosity. If she ever got a whiff of the gossip that
the Snyders might be making moonshine whiskey
in that old house, he was afraid that his granddaughter would get curious enough to go poking her nose
around, hoping she might see the still in operation.

So Taffy played with Brandy and her friends on
the sandhills close by the shack. The dog tagged
her footsteps, obeying her every command. Taffy felt
the restrictions her grandfather placed on her. No
longer did she feel free as the sandpipers flitting
across the beach. But she didn't rebel, knowing that
Gramp always did what he thought best for her.

Big Jens or some of the station crew still came by the shack every weekend to pick up mullets. Gramp would walk out to the jeep sometimes, and he and Big Jens would talk for fifteen or twenty minutes. Taffy began to notice how they stopped talking or changed the subject suddenly if she happened to walk their way. It puzzled her.

"Gramp hasn't acted right since the day the Japs bombed Pearl Harbor," she thought. "That was the day he went over to Sam Mills' house," she remembered. "He was silent and strange at supper that night, as if he had something deep on his mind. Well, what I don't know won't hurt me, I reckon."

She watched the jeeps and coast guard trucks go up and down the beach. Evenings, just before dark, she saw the patrols and their dogs take their places at their beach stations. She watched from a distance as a construction gang put up the big steel tower near the point of the Cape. After she went to bed at night, she watched the beams of the light tower in Buxton woods as they revolved and swiveled over the dark ocean. Even with the blackouts all over the coasts, the tall, skeleton tower still threw out its light to any and all mariners who might be passing the shoals of the dangerous North Carolina cape. Taffy's life was not exactly dull, but war was leaving its depressing mark.

It was sometime in the latter part of June that Malene came to spend the night with her.

"Mamma nearly had a fit when I asked her. Said I'd crowd you to death out here in the shack," Malene giggled, brushing her hair.

"Shucks, no," Taffy affirmed. "My cot is a wide one. It'll hold us just fine."

"Well, she let me come. Golly, I always wondered how it would feel to sleep so close to the ocean. Our house sits away off over in the village."

"That old sea just rocks you right to sleep," Taffy told her.

"Do you ever go on the beach at night?"

"Not for a long time. Big Jens told me not to, and Gramp has forbidden it. I don't know why, though. Seems like it would be safe enough with all the patrols out now."

"Yeah. But they haven't got enough men to cover every inch of that beach, you know. Those patrols are about eight miles apart, aren't they?"

"Something like that."

"Maybe Big Jens and your grandfather are scared something would happen to you."

"Well, Gramp gets real angry if I say anything about wanting to peep out there at night. Gee whiz, that's when the ocean is prettiest. At night."

"Well, that does it," Malene said. "One hundred swipes with the brush. Mamma says this mop of hair always looks like the wild man from Borneo. I'm ready for bed, if you are. So go ahead and blow out the light. Can you raise the shades after you blow it out?"

"Sure. I do it all the time. With my window right on that side of the bed, I can lie there and look out over the ocean every night. There's a low dent in the sand fence opposite my window, so I can see the ocean real plain."

"Will you let me lie on that side so I can look out?"

"Sure," Taffy agreed. "I can watch any old night."

"Guess what Penelope Etheridge told me the other day?" Malene whispered.

"What?"

"A patrol found a rubber boat on the beach between Hatteras and Ocracoke."

"No!"

"Yes, they did. Penny's pop is stationed down there. And he knows. He saw it. It was hid in a clump of palmettos."

"Where do they think it came from?"

"Submarine, silly. Saboteurs put it ashore, I'll bet!"

"Golly," Taffy shivered. Saboteurs that close? It wasn't a pleasant thought. But why would saboteurs be landing on these lonely sand beaches?

Gramp Morgan was snoring in the next room. Malene giggled. "Gramp sure is sawing wood."

"He does that all the time," Taffy yawned. "Sometimes I have to get up and go jiggle him to make him turn over so I can go to sleep."

Malene yawned and turned over facing the window. The night was cloudy and very humid. The moon had not risen. A haze overspread the sky, giving it a summer murkiness. Taffy twisted and turned, trying to get comfortable.

"Taffy, look!" Malene nudged her. "Raise up and look at that light! It's gone! There it is again!" Malene breathed excitedly.

"Probably one of the patrols going by," Taffy told her, raising herself unconcernedly.

"No sir. It's on the water, way out there," Malene

pointed. "See? There it is again."

Both girls pressed their noses against the wire screen. Sure enough there it was—a white light, low over the sea. It came, and in a second it was gone. The sea was smooth, so the light shone very clearly when it appeared.

"What do you reckon it is?" Taffy whispered, really excited now that she sensed something peculiar about the situation.

"Let's get on our clothes and sneak out to the beach and see."

"Gosh, I don't know," Taffy breathed. Nothing in the world would suit her any better. But if Gramp were to wake up and find her gone, he'd be awful mad. She didn't like to be disobedient. Then if one of the patrols caught them, no telling what would happen. Big Jens would have a fit too. Temptation and conscience pulled a tug of war. Temptation won. "I'll get Brandy," she whispered, pulling on her blue jeans and shirt as she tiptoed out. "You be awful quiet," she cautioned Malene.

The children closed the door softly. Gramp Morgan was still snoring peacefully. "You hold the flashlight. We might need it," Taffy instructed. "I've got Brandy on his leash. He doesn't like a leash, so I'll have to kinda hold him down. Quiet, boy. We're going to the beach." The dog seemed to sense the excitement of the children, but he walked quietly beside them as they cat-footed through the sand.

They went over the first sand fence. About five hundred feet away were low scrub oaks and yaupon bushes and a tangled thicket of Spanish bayonet growing close to the water's edge.

"Let's get behind these bushes and watch," Malene whispered. "If a patrol happens to go by, he won't see us."

"Steady, feller." Taffy rubbed the big boxer's nose. "Come on and sit down here by me." Brandy sat, but he strained on the leash. It was an unaccustomed hindrance and he didn't like it one bit. But he obeyed.

"There it is again," Malene whispered, pointing in the darkness.

"Yeah, I see it. It goes and comes quick, doesn't it?"

"Looks like it's getting farther offshore."

"Don't know. Seems to be gone altogether now."

A jeep roared down the beach. Brandy whined

softly. "Quiet, boy!" Taffy commanded. The dog growled low in his throat. "Quiet, I say. You don't want us to get caught, do you?" Brandy licked Taffy's cheek.

"Wonder if that patrol saw the light? Must not have, because he's still going up the beach."

"It's about time to change the watch," Taffy whispered. "One patrol meets another farther up the beach. Sometimes they talk for a few minutes before the relieved guard goes back to the station."

"Listen! Did you hear something?"

"Nope. Nothing but the surf."

"Sounded like something being dragged . . . kind of a whooshing sound."

"Let's move over toward the end of the palmettos. Maybe we can hear it again."

It was a thousand wonders that they didn't get pricked a dozen times with the sharp palmetto blades as they moved silently through the sand. Brandy muttered deep in his throat. Taffy could feel the quivering of his flesh. Her own nerves were getting taut.

"Golly, Moses! Look, Malene! Out there near the waterline, over toward that dune. It's a man. And he's dragging something. See, he's all bent down."

Malene strained her eyes in the dark. "Sh," she cautioned, pinching Taffy. "Hear that sound? Like the faraway tolling of a bell?"

"Yeah, I hear it. What are we going to do?"

"We're going to stay right here and watch and listen. I'm too scared to move anyway. Gee whillikins, you know what's going on out there, don't you?"

"Sure, I reckon I do," Taffy gulped, not liking the situation they had got themselves into. The dog began pulling to get away. "Sh, Brandy, quiet." But the growls got stronger. "I can't hold him," Taffy gasped. "He's gone! What shall we do?"

"Let's get out of here. Right now," Malene chattered. "This is no place for us. Come on. Hurry!"

"Not without my dog," Taffy gasped stubbornly, taking off after Brandy like a streak of lightning. The tangled vines, the low-lying yaupon scrub, and the darkness made her way difficult; but she ran in the general direction where she and Malene had seen the man disappear on the beach. She could hear Malene scrambling through the underbrush. "Brandy," Taffy called, "here, Brandy!" Immediately a low growl answered her. It sounded very near. "Here, boy," she wheedled, her body shaking with a nervous chill. "Where are you?"

Suddenly she felt herself grabbed from behind. A hand went over her mouth before she could utter a scream for help. In a split second, Brandy sprang through the scrub and attacked. The big dog knocked Taffy and the man sprawling. The man let out a blood-curdling yell and let go of Taffy as the dog grabbed him.

"Hold him, Brandy, hold him!" Taffy screamed at the top of her lungs, picking herself up out of the sand. With bared teeth, the dog stood over the prostrate man—ferocity in every inch of his big body. The man fought to protect his throat.

"Help! Help!" Malene's screams added to the din.

A jeep came flying down the beach. Soon it was close enough for its dimmed lights to shine on the dog and man wrestling on the sand.

"Hold him, boy! Hold him!" Taffy continued to yell.

In a matter of seconds, the area was full of patrols and armed guards.

Big Jens' voice cut through the night. "What's

going on here? Girls, what's the meaning of this? Call off the dog, Taffy," he commanded. The big Norwegian yanked the man up off the sand. "Now give an account of yourself," he said, shoving him hard up against a dune. "Who are you? Where'd you come from? What are you doing out here?" Big Jens held him penned against the dune.

The man muttered something unintelligible in a low guttural voice.

Brandy's flesh quivered under Taffy's hand; his bristles stood on end.

"So? You're one of them, eh?" Big Jens snarled. "Well, we've got just the place for you and your kind. Give me those handcuffs, Mills." The chief slipped the manacles on the man slick as grease. He patted him up and down his body, searching for firearms. "Nice little gun you got here in this shoulder holster." He passed the pistol to one of the patrols. "Take care of that," he told him. An armed guard held a steady gun on the prisoner.

"Look, Chief," one of the patrols called, shining his light. "Looks like he came prepared to blow up the whole island and then some." There, lying on the sand about five feet away, was a big box. It was plainly marked DYNAMIT. Big Jens swore under his breath.

"Don't fool with that box," he warned quickly. "We need the benefit of daylight to examine it. No telling what sort of booby traps are in it. Besides that, it's not our job to open it. We'll guard it till the proper authorities come. Hanson, Josephson, Mills, take over guard duty here till daylight. Maury, Jones, Fulcher, guard this man till I walk the girls back to the shack. And you, Mr. Saboteur, you're headed for a date with Uncle Sam's boys. May the Lord have mercy on your soul!"

Big Jens put his arms around the shaking girls and briskly walked them toward the shack. Taffy held tight to Brandy.

"What in the name of Ned were you kids doing on the beach?" he asked sternly. "Taffy, I'm surprised at you. I don't like it. You hear me?"

"Yes, sir," Taffy hung her head. "Gramp was asleep. He didn't know about our coming."

"We saw a funny-looking light," Malene began, "after we had gone to bed, and . . ."

"It was white and low on the sea, and it kept going off and on, so we . . ."

"So we took Brandy and slipped out to see what it was," Malene finished.

"We heard a bell tolling too," Taffy told him.

"Yeah. Probably had a buddy who set him ashore in a rubber boat. The bell tolled on the sub so his buddy could find his way back." Big Jens wiped his face with a big bandanna. "I've been going to sea for nigh on to thirty years, but never have I seen anything to equal it. Two kids and a dog catching an enemy agent. Yes, sir, it beats me."

"It beats me too," Malene gulped. "Mamma is going to whale the daylights out of me when she hears about it."

"Golly, I don't know what Gramp will do with me," Taffy sobbed softly in her nervousness.

"It's a thousand wonders you didn't get shot," the skipper told them sternly. "Things I've been wondering about are beginning . . ." The skipper stopped, thinking better of what he had started to say.

"I'll see if Gramp's awake."

But Gramp was still snoring.

"He hasn't even turned over," Taffy whispered. "He's still sawing gourds just like he was when we left."

"You kids get in that house and go to bed," Big Jens told them. "And don't you ever go on that beach again at night as long as this war's going on. I shudder to think what could have happened out there tonight. But with all my fussing, I'm right proud of you. You two and that boxer dog did a good turn for your country this night. Go on to bed now. I'll see you tomorrow morning." Big Jens went muttering into the night. "Dangdest thing I ever saw," he mumbled, taking the sand fences in giant strides.

Needless to say, the girls didn't sleep a wink. It seemed hours before they stopped trembling. Then they debated how to tell Gramp and Malene's mother.

"I got to tell him myself," Taffy worried. "He'll hear it anyway. So I'd better be the one."

"Jiminy gosh, will I catch it, when Mamma hears about this!" Malene chattered. "But I reckon it'll be worth a licking. Yeah, I reckon I won't mind a licking too much," she yawned sleepily. "But I was never so scared in my life."

"You can say that again," Taffy mumbled from under the pillow.

7. Brandy Gets Decorated

Taffy and Malene were up at the crack of dawn and had eaten breakfast long before Gramp Morgan awoke. Before Gramp could get his clothes on, Big Jens drove up in the jeep!

"Any mullets this morning?" the chief called.

"What in tarnation is goin' on araound here?" Gramp scolded. "What's everybody doin' up so early?" He could smell the boiling coffee and knew that Taffy was up ahead of him. He couldn't understand it. And Big Jens, what was he after mullets for? He ought to know it was too early to go fishing, and besides, it wasn't even his day to get fish. Gramp hurried into his clothes and made his way out to the back door.

Brandy ran from the shack and jumped up on Big Jens, licking his hands.

"Down, old boy," Big Jens laughed, patting the boxer. "I'm not a saboteur!"

"He'd nail you good-fashion, if you were," Gramp blinked, wiping off his bifocals. "What in thunder are you after mullets this soon in the mornin' for? Oi thought you told me the missus wouldn't cook fish for breakfast," Gramp went on. "Besoides that, Oi ain't fished yet."

"I don't want mullets, Gramp." The chief grinned lopsidedly. "Thought I'd better come over early and help Taffy and Malene tell you how they and Brandy caught an enemy spy on the beach last night!"

Gramp looked stunned. He bugged his eyes and grabbed Big Jens by the arm. "What in blazes are you talkin' abaout? Enemy spoy? Taffy and Malene? Where? How?" Gramp looked at the girls severely. So that was the reason for all the early rising and smartness this morning.

The story came out. And it was difficult to know who was more excited in the telling, Big Jens or the girls. Brandy ran up and down from first one to the other, wanting to share in the excitement.

"Yes, sir," Big Jens went on, "that submarine crew had things timed perfectly. Right when the guards were changing watch about five miles up the beach. That's when the spy sneaked ashore. It beats me how they knew the time so well. There's something funny about that. He looked knowingly at Gramp. Gramp frowned and shook his head in bewilderment. The expression on Big Jens' face showed that the incident would be investigated a lot more before it became a closed issue. "Anyway," he went on talking to Gramp, "if it hadn't been for the girls' curiosity and that dog, no telling what things might look like on the island this morning. Why, man alive, there was enough dynamite in that box to blow us to kingdom-come. Just a little bit of it would have knocked out every government installation on the island."

"Maybe he was goin' to use the other dynamite someplace else," Gramp volunteered.

"Yeah, either that or he brought it ashore for somebody else to use," Big Jens said grimly. Taffy gave Malene a very puzzled look. Malene shrugged her shoulders, not knowing either.

Gramp Morgan wiped his eyes and blew his nose.

"Well, sir, it beats anythin' Oi ever heard of in moy loife," he sniffed. "Taffy, Oi ought to give you a good thrashin' for goin' to that beach, and you too, Malene. Scares me plum to death, it does, naow that it's all done and over with. Oi reckon Sal Oden will have somethin' to talk abaout naow for the rest of her borned days!"

Malene giggled. Big Jens roared. But Taffy squirmed, remembering how old Mrs. Oden always picked at her. "Hope she doesn't ever hear about it," Taffy said miserably.

"I'm thinking everybody will be mighty proud of what these girls did," Big Jens said. Brandy sat up on his hind legs and offered the chief a paw. "Yeah, and you too, old fellow," Big Jens told the boxer, rubbing his silky ears. "Reckon I'll just have to decorate you myself." The chief slipped his hand into his pocket and pulled out a silver chain with a medallion on it. He snapped it around the dog's neck. "Go show it to Taffy," he commanded.

Brandy trotted over and sat down on his haunches.

"Oh," Taffy squealed rapturously, "it's a chain with a life-saving medal on it. What a fine collar it makes, Brandy!"

"Looks just like a fair jewel a-shining in the sun," Malene exclaimed, lifting it up.

"Naow it sure does," Gramp nodded. "And Oi reckon you earned it fair and square from what Big Jens says," Gramp added, patting Brandy's head.

"Oh, yes, Malene, I stopped by your house on the way down and told your mamma. She promised me she wouldn't whale the daylights out of you this time," Big Jens told her.

"Golly, Moses, I'm glad to hear that," Malene said soberly. "I thought sure I'd catch it. Bet I would've too if you hadn't stopped and told her. Reckon I won't be scared any more now."

"Wish I could say the same thing," the skipper sighed. "Guess I'm more afraid right now than at any time since I've been on the island." Big Jens walked over and got into the jeep. He waved as he drove off.

"Now what do you reckon he meant by that?" Malene said curiously. "Big Jens hasn't ever been scared of anything."

"Naow never you moind what he meant," Gramp told the girls sternly, worrying to himself about what the chief had said. "There's strange goin's-on here on this oisland, and the least we know and see the better off we'll be. You never moind abaout what Big Jens meant. That's his business. And you young-uns stay off that beach from naow on. Oi mean what Oi say, Taffy Willis, or Oi'll take a waterbush switch to you."

Taffy nodded dejectedly. The girls walked over to the bench under the oak tree and sat down. "See, what did I tell you?" Taffy groaned. "He won't even want me to step my little toe out there even in the daytime from now on."

"Reckon we'll have to cook up some excitement in the Cape woods this summer," Malene sighed. "As if anything important ever happened in those pines!" she said scornfully, looking out over the green stretch of trees in Buxton village.

"Yeah, isn't that so?" Taffy agreed. "Summer won't be like summer at all without the ocean. Guess Manteo jail couldn't be worse."

"Well, we can explore Trent woods." Malene brightened. "There are some wonderful places for picnics down there. And also some high sandhills. Maybe we'll see some of those little deer the conservation department turned loose. Of course, there'll be squirrels and rabbits to see."

Taffy looked out at the ocean, thinking of the tameness of squirrels and rabbits after helping to catch a saboteur! "Guess Brandy will like going in the woods, roaming around. Bet he'll chase the rabbits something awful. Then, too, we can go clamming and scalloping, and soft crabbing on the Sound side. Nothing's been said about us going there. Gramp still fishes out there in the daytime."

"Clamming's fun," Malene told her. "Besides, we can swim in the Sound too, provided the wind's right, so the nettles won't sting us to death." Taffy nodded, remembering the hundreds of times that she had been set on fire by the stings of the jellyfish, which the islanders called sea nettles. Gentle north winds brought the jellyfish by thousands close to the Sound shore. "Taffy," Malene said, suddenly changing the subject, "what do you reckon Big Jens meant awhile ago when he was leaving?"

"I can't imagine," Taffy said, looking up sharply. "Do you think he believes that there's somebody . . ."

"Gosh!" Malene gasped. "I know just what you're thinking. But who?"

"Sh," Taffy cautioned. "Gramp's coming. Let's

get Sailor and ride down to your house and get your horse. We'll gallop down through the village and back. We can talk then."

"I know. Ask Gramp to let you spend the day with me. We'll go crabbing down at Lem's landing."

"That'll be fine if he'll let me go. But he probably won't let me out for a month."

"Well, ask him," Malene commanded.

"Gramp, can I spend the day with Malene?" Taffy shouted. "I won't go to the beach and I'll mind this time."

Gramp scratched his head, thinking whether to let her or not. Finally he gave in. "Oi reckon you can," he hollered back. "But you be sure to get home a long toime before dark. Remember all the things Oi been tellin' you. You goin' to roide Sailor?"

"Yes, sir."

"Well, Oi'll keep Brandy. Want to take him fishin' with me."

"Can Taffy eat dinner and stay long enough for us to have a crab roast this evening?" Malene begged. "Please, Gramp Morgan. It gets lonesome now that we can't play on the beach any more."

"Yep. Oi don't care if she does. But moind you, see

that you get home before dark," Gramp insisted. "And behave yourself."

Taffy promised, already on her way to get Sailor.

"Land of Goshen!" Malene gasped. "I plum forgot I let my brother ride my pony up to Kinnakeet today."

"Don't worry," Taffy told her. "Why, Sailor could take us both a hundred miles and never feel it."

So the two happy youngsters mounted the Banks pony and went galloping over the sand dunes towards Malene's house in the village, both of them forgetting about the super secret they had planned to talk about, and Taffy never dreaming what the end of the day would bring.

8. Discovery!

Big Jens was worried. All the way to the lookout post by Creeds Hill Coast Guard Station he had been thinking about the happenings during the last twenty-four hours.

"There is something definitely rotten in the good state of Denmark," he told himself. "But what is it? How could a submarine at sea know when my boys were going to change the guard on the beach? The thing was planned to the minute. And why all that dynamite? There's just one answer. There's treachery on this island. Somebody, operating under cover, is supplying information to the enemy. And I believe I know who. But how shall I prove it? That's the question. How to get evidence." The chief applied brakes and turned the jeep off the beach, gunning the vehicle down the serpentine tracks toward the village of Hatteras.

In a few minutes, he turned out of the woods west of the Cape, where the road passed sandhills thickly timbered with loblolly pine, live oak, and yaupon. The trees inclined westward, bent by the winds which continually swept the Cape.

"Got to get old man Lawson to cure me some more yaupon. Sure beats store-bought tea a mile," he was thinking as he pulled up at the lookout post. An armed guard was on duty. He saluted the chief smartly.

"Everything O.K., Bill?"

"Yes, sir, Chief," Bill grinned. "Had to do a little work on my squawk-box this morning. This dampness down here kind of corrodes the batteries."

"Yeah, I know. Things are quiet, eh? Nothing to report? Telephone lines all right?"

"Everything is in order, sir. But I just talked to Johansen—he's on duty in the radio shack down at the DF Station—he said he just picked up a peculiar kind of signal. Said he couldn't identify it at all." The skipper pricked up his ears.

"What kind of signal was it?" Big Jens asked, his interest mounting. "How'd he describe it?"

"Well, sir, he said it sounded and acted like a short wave or high frequency or something. Said he'd searched the books for all kinds of call signals, and that one he couldn't make out at all. It wasn't a distress signal. Just a peculiar sort of thing. Asked me if I knew of anybody on the island who was a ham operator. I told him nobody on the island had a set except Jody Oden, and he sold his to one of the station crew when he went overseas. That set's down at the station right now all dismantled where the boys have been working on it."

Big Jens listened intently. Things began popping in his mind. Loose ends tied together, and answers started coming. He looked at his watch. It was nearly noon.

"Thanks, Bill," Big Jens said without batting an eye. "Guess I'd better get back for chow. There's your relief coming right now. See you at the station."

Big Jens ran to the jeep and gunned the motor to life. He took off over the sand dunes like a deer running for cover.

"Golly," Bill marveled, "one of these days the chief

is going to break his neck in that thing. Wonder what he's in such an all-fired hurry for?"

Down through Trent woods Big Jens tore in the jeep, straightening out old tracks and making new ones through the narrow trail. His mind was in a turmoil. He had been stupid and blind.

"Why, I am naive as a baby. Should have looked into all that village gossip about moonshine stills." He gritted his teeth. "Here I am in charge of a big government installation, and it's my business to know everything that goes on on this island. Me a-warning Gramp and Taffy about things, and here I have been blind as a bat. Moonshiners, my maiden aunt! The whole thing is as plain as daylight. It's got to be the answer."

He swung out of the woods on to the open beach. Just before he reached the village, he headed the jeep toward the trail which led to the unused back road near the Snyder house. He stopped the jeep about five hundred feet away and got out. Cautiously keeping himself hidden in the low scrub oaks and yaupon, he walked toward the house.

"Yeah," he said, stopping to peer through the bushes, "that's the answer all right. Been staring us in the face for months. Just look at that framework on the chimney! It's peculiar-looking all right. Boiled right down to plain hard facts, that's a super-duper short wave outfit tuned to every Nazi submarine frequency in the Atlantic Ocean. But there's more to it. How do they get the information they shortwave to the subs? Could it be possible that . . . No! There couldn't be any traitors among my radio operators. I am sure of that. I know all my boys too well. No, the leak in the information is farther up the line somewhere. Whatever the set-up, this Snyder house is part of the answer. And now, Kenneth Freuchen Jens, prize dope of all Scandihoovians—who ought to be tied to an Arctic iceberg and set adrift in the Skagerrak for being so blind—get yourself back to that jeep and to the DF Station where you can grab a telephone and get some Top Brass in on this thing. And fast!"

The big Norwegian cat-footed back through the scrub to the jeep. In seconds he was off through the thicket, the vehicle scattering a covey of quail before it. "Out of my way, Bob Whites!" he said grimly. "I've got other birds to pluck right now. And every one of them has a black swastika around his neck!"

9. Danger!

Taffy and Malene spent the day crabbing and playing along the Sound shore. Late in the afternoon Lorrie and Kenny joined them.

"Hey, you're just in time to help gather driftwood for the crab roast," Taffy called.

"Shucks," Kenny protested, "it's too hot to build a fire."

"You're just too lazy," Malene accused him.

"Aw, dry up," Kenny told her, grinning. "You just feel all puffed up about helping to catch that spy last night. Gosh, wish I'd been with you girls. Boy, I bet that Nazi was really petrified when Brandy jumped on him." Kenny hadn't forgotten the day when Brandy had flattened him on the sand.

Taffy laughed. "He sure got him all right. Worse

than he got you that day."

"Something sure is popping around the DF Station this afternoon," Kenny told them. "Pop's been telephoning 'way over an hour. I heard him in the radio shack. One of the guards saw me listening and chased me off. And just before I left, an airplane landed on the beach right in front of the Station. You ought to have seen the navy 'brass' unloading. There were some men in civilian clothes too. Pop scooted me off. Told me to get lost. Looks like he wanted to get rid of me for some reason. Something's cooking. Wish I knew what. I know it's got something to do with what happened last night. But I can't figure out what."

"Gosh, Taffy, do you reckon all that navy's come to court-martial you and me?" Malene gasped.

"For goodness sakes, what for?" Kenny demanded. "Don't you even know what a court-martial is? It's some kind of court where they try you for crimes. It's no crime to catch a spy, is it? For gosh sakes, girls are dumb!"

"All right, Mr. Smartypants, throw some driftwood on that fire if you want a hard crab to eat," Malene snapped.

For some reason Taffy wasn't enjoying the crab roast as much as usual. She had an uneasy feeling about something that got stronger with the increasing darkness. Goose chills began to run up and down her spine—even though it wasn't cold a bit on the Sound shore. Her mind was whirling with the things Kenny had told them. What was Big Jens up to? Just then, over to the left, among the water myrtles by Joad Gray's landing, she heard a noise like something breaking bushes.

"What was that?" Kenny suddenly straightened up, holding a hard crab by the claw.

"Don't know," Taffy said quietly, her heart in her throat.

"Probably Joad's beagle hound chasing a rabbit," Malene told them unconcernedly.

"Well, I'm going to call up Sailor before he wanders off," Taffy told them, whistling through her fingers. The horse came trotting. She tied him to a nearby stump.

"I'm for getting home," Lorrie told the children emphatically. "I don't like funny noises in the bushes that a body can't see. Makes me think of old Polly the Witch that haunts this end of the island. Let's get this fire put out right now. Boy, that sun sure went down fast, didn't it? I'm getting chilly, too. Let's get a move on. It's almost dark!"

"Yeah," Kenny agreed, worriedly surveying the area with his keen blue eyes. "Sitting around the fire here, we didn't notice."

"Golly, I better get home," Taffy said anxiously, remembering her promise to Gramp. "Come on, let's get this fire put out. Hurry!"

The children shoveled sand with their hands and covered the live coals of the fire. Kenny picked up an old bucket and dipped water from the Sound and threw it over the fire. Then they kicked more sand over the wetness.

"That's got it," Lorrie said. "Malene, let's you and Kenny and I wade down to our landing instead of going across the marsh. Too many sand spurs that way. And it's too dark to see them before we step on them with our bare feet."

"Yeah, that's right," Malene agreed.

"Suits me," Kenny said. "I'm not hankering to get my feet full of thorns tonight."

Taffy ran for her horse. She should have left sooner. She hadn't meant to disobey Gramp. He'd be madder than a hornet and worried about her not being home before dark.

"I'll take the short cut down the old back road," she said to herself. "I can cut off over a mile that way." So great was her anxiety to get home that she never remembered that Gramp had forbidden her to use the back road. She waved to the children and turned Sailor over the marsh. "Go, boy," she nudged him.

By the time she came to the edge of the thicket, it was quite dark. Sailor galloped his sure-footed way through the darkness of the pines that edged the old road past the Snyder house. The trail was narrow and the trees set up black shadows like tall giants. Suddenly Sailor snorted and seemed to stumble. Taffy felt herself hurled head-over-heels over the horse's body into the side of a tree, and then into the sand, the breath nearly knocked out of her. Consciousness left her as a horrible smothering sensation completely enveloped her.

Two dark figures scurried around the prostrate girl, wrapping the blanket securely about her.

"Quick. Get that strand of wire off the trees from across the trail," one of them directed the other.

"It broke in two when the horse hit it," the other replied.

"Never mind. Inside the gate!"

They picked up Taffy and ran, carrying the unconscious girl like a sack of meal. The gate swung to and the lock clicked. The front door of the old house opened, and the two men disappeared, carrying Taffy inside.

"This will teach Miss Busybody to mind her own business," a guttural voice said.

"Ja. Your plan worked like a charm. All that snooping you did watching those kids this afternoon paid off. But you couldn't be sure she'd take the old road home, or that it would even be dark when she started," an older man told him.

"Ja. Lady Luck smiled on us. If the Willis girl hadn't come this way tonight, she would have sooner or later. I am a patient man. I'd have got her sooner or later."

"I don't like this, Holstein," a third man, younger than the others, spoke. He was a tall, blond giant.

"You worry too much, Hans. You let old Blountz Holstein handle it. I'll take care of the situation. This girl knows too much."

The eldest man spoke again. "She and that dog surely upset things last night. We've no way of knowing whether the navy wormed any information out of Lieberstein or not. He's been trained to stay silent. It's been nearly twenty-four hours now. If he had talked, I feel sure they'd have been after us before this—that they'd have been watching this house. We can't take any chances. We've got to move fast now. Get out of here for good. Tonight! That navy and coast guard outfit might get suspicious in a hurry."

"Is the girl dead?" Hans asked, bending over Taffy and unwrapping the blanket.

"No. Just knocked out from the fall. We'd better tie her up. She'll be coming to any minute. Gag her and blindfold her. We can't have her complicating things further."

They tied Taffy securely and shoved her in a corner of the big room.

"What about her horse?" Hans asked.

"He went flying toward the beach. He's probably swimming Hatteras Inlet by now."

"The pony might have gone home," the blond giant continued. "I don't like it. We haven't enough time. We'll never get away with this, I tell you."

"Hans Snyder, you are very trying to the patience," the older man said. "Here we have operated all winter and spring right under the noses of these stupid islanders and a whole beach full of navy and coast guard men. Early in the winter, gossip got around in the village that there might be some bootlegging going on in this house. That was fine. When they talked about that, they never thought of anything else. Not even the radio crew at the DF Station have questioned the radio antenna. Besides, the simple fools around this island think our house has been empty for three months or more. Stupid pigs! So why do you complain and fret? We've done our work well. *Der Fuehrer* is proud of us." He fondled an Iron Cross which lay on the desk. "Over twenty Allied ships we've helped to send to the bottom off these shores. Ja, there's been real teamwork between us, the U-boats, and our agents farther north. Last night's events are very unfortunate, thanks to the meddling of this stupid girl and her dog!"

"I still don't like it, Father." Hans shook his head Taffy moaned. "She's coming to," he whispered frantically. "She'll have the whole village **down on** us before we can get away."

"You sniveling ox," Holstein snapped. "Get **busy** and saturate this radio equipment with gasoline. I'll see to it that the girl stays quiet. Hand me **that can** of chloroform and a sponge, Herr Snyder. **Get that** gag out of her mouth. We'll see how much **yelling** she can do after a few whiffs of this. Little Miss Busybody is going to take a nice, long snooze. Maybe she won't even wake up at all." Taffy lay pale and still as the big German held the chloroform sponge over her nose and mouth. "There!" Holstein clicked his heels. "Heil Hitler!"

10. Big Jens Comes Through

Gramp sat on the back stoop waiting. The sun was down and darkness was falling fast over the Cape. Taffy hadn't come home, and Gramp was beginning to worry. He didn't know what had got into his granddaughter lately. It wasn't like her to be disobedient. "Reckon she's just growin' up and gettin' a little bit rambunctious," he said to Brandy. "She'll be home in a minute or two. Maybe the younguns just forgot the toime when they were roastin' crabs. Think Oi'll turn on the radio and see if the summer static will let up enough for me to hear the war news."

Still Taffy didn't come.

At eight-thirty, Gramp heard Sailor tearing over the sand fence.

"Oi'll sure give Taffy Willis a lacin' out she won't forget in a hurry," Gramp muttered, stepping firmly out the kitchen door. "Say, young lady, didn't Oi tell you to get home before dark? Where you been this late?"

Sailor came trotting to Gramp, snorting savagely.

"Whoy, where's Taffy?" the old man exclaimed. The horse snorted again and pawed the ground.

"Oi'll bet you've throwed her, you frisky devil," Gramp fumed. "Oi knowed you'd do it some day. Can't trust you Banks ponies ten seconds. Come on, Brandy," Gramp called to the dog. "We got to go foind Taffy." The boxer came bounding at the sound of Taffy's name. "Oi hope that miserable hoss didn't throw her against a tree," the old man worried. "Come on, Brandy. We'll go to the lookaout post on the beach first. That guard's got a walkie-talkie. Oi'll get him to call Big Jens to come in the jeep to help me foind her. Poor little thing. She may be hurt bad. Dag nab hoss. Hallo, there," Gramp hollered, plowing his way through the sand. "Hallo, aout there. It's Gramp. And Oi need help!"

"What's wrong, Gramp? the guard yelled back.

"It's Taffy. Sailor just come home withaout her. That pesky hoss has throwed her and she's layin' somewhere hurt. Call Big Jens to come. Tell him to hurry." Gramp Morgan paced the sand in the darkness, rubbing his hands nervously.

"Sure, Gramp," the guard said, calling the DF Station. "Hey, Joe, get Big Jens down to Gramp's shack on the double. Taffy's horse has thrown her somewhere on the dunes and Gramp needs help to find her . . . What's that? . . . Big Jens not at the station? Who is? . . . Well, roust them out of their bunks and tell them to get here quick! . . . Yeah, post 17 . . . That's right . . . and tell them to hurry!" The guard put the receiver back on its hook.

"Big Jens isn't at the station, Gramp. There's nobody there except the radio operators on duty, two men who've just gone to bed off watches, and one guard. Johansen said the coast guard truck left the station half an hour ago loaded with the station crew. Can't imagine what's up. Johnson and Stiles are coming on the ambulance to help you look for Taffy. That must be the jeep turning out on the beach now."

◆ ◆ ◆ ◆ ◆ ◆ ◆ ◆

Big Jens, naval intelligence, and FBI men planned careful strategy that summer afternoon. Every possible angle was worked out, and men were detailed. They would wait for the darkness.

The chief prayed that nothing would go wrong, that the whole miserable business could be accomplished without the islanders knowing anything about it until it was all over. They had trouble enough; and there was always a danger that somebody, however inadvertently, might give the alarm.

Darkness fell rapidly over the Cape woods. About half a mile from the thicket on the back road, two jeeps and a coast guard truck came to a stop.

"Fan out, men," the chief directed. "Completely surround the house. Each of you knows what to do. Remember we must get inside that house. Synchronize your watches. It's exactly twenty forty-five. At twenty-one hundred we close in. Remember, you are dealing with enemy agents. It will be your life against theirs. You have guns. Shoot if you have to. Take them alive if possible. That's all. Let's go!"

Like shadows in a dark forest, Big Jens and his men made their way stealthily to the old boarded-up house on the knoll. The chief and Joe Beasley, Seaman 1st class, led the way. The light, aluminum ladder they carried was set against the fence. Sure-footed as cats, they went over. Behind them came nearly a dozen men. They spread out and began to converge on the old house.

"Sh," Big Jens cautioned, touching Joe. Subdued voices were coming from somewhere to the rear of the house. The chief and Joe made their silent way through the sand until they were almost directly behind the persons hidden in the darkness.

"I tell you, it's a foolish thing to do." A voice spoke low. "We'll never get away with it. Holstein's temper will ruin us yet. His idea of getting even with the Willis girl is no good, I tell you. Besides, it's foolish to try to destroy that equipment with fire. It won't burn, no matter how much we soak it with gasoline. We can't get rid of the evidence that way."

"Hans Snyder, you complain like an old woman," his father snapped. "Can't you understand that this place is useless to us now; that it has served its purpose? Hurry and soak the porch with that gasoline. Throw some of it over in the grass too. Once we touch a match here, I want it to go up like a tinder box. A speedboat is waiting. Before these islanders discover the equipment, we'll be well on our way across Pamlico Sound, headed for the mainland. Our friend will have our car ready. Like Blountz says, you worry too much. You've got to have a spine of steel in our business. Besides, nobody is going to connect us with this night's doings. These stupid islanders think the old place has been uninhabited for three months. The navy and coast guard certainly don't suspect us, or they'd have made a move before now. We've covered our tracks completely."

"But, Father, I don't like leaving that Willis girl to burn up. That's murder!"

"Why, the dirty------, they've got Taffy in there!" Big Jens whispered in horror. This was a development the chief had not counted on. Joe nudged his commanding officer to silence.

"You stupid ox," the father snarled. "What's so different about the girl? She's an American swine like the others, isn't she? Have you forgotten Herr Lieberstein and what happened to him last night?

You saw her boxer dog jump him. You know what will probably become of him. And all because of that girl! Where's all the toughness you were supposed to acquire five years ago in that training camp in the Fatherland? Let the Willis girl fry! What you need is some of *Der Fuehrer's* discipline, and when we get back to Baltimore, I'm going to see that . . ."

Whatever it was the elder Snyder was going to say was cut off by the very simple expedient of Big Jens' ham-like hands closing over the man's windpipe. Simultaneously his son, Hans, felt the muzzle of a gun shoved against the back of his head.

"One yap, and you're a dead duck, you stinking Nazi." The chief grated his teeth. Snyder struggled to get out of the smothering grasp. It was useless. With one hand, Big Jens held the agent by the throat. With the other, he delivered a short blow to the chin that knocked the gasping Nazi into temporary unconsciousness.

"Open your mouth, and I'll blow you to kingdom-come!" Joe Beasley hissed through his teeth. He spun the young Nazi around with a solid clip to his ear. Hans fell. Joe was on him in a split second.

In a matter of minutes, Big Jens and Joe had

bound and gagged both men and dragged them over to the side of the fence where armed guards were hidden. "Blast their insides out, if they make a sound," Big Jens commanded through clenched teeth. The odor of gasoline had begun to creep into the hot, muggy night. "Come on, Joe, we haven't time to warn the others about Taffy. There's not a second to lose. Any minute, somebody in that house may strike a match.

The chief was frantic. Taffy was somewhere in the old house. How she got there and in what condition she was he did not know. He had to find her. And fast! But he had to be careful. He didn't know how many more enemy agents were inside the house. He didn't know the interior arrangements. Breaking through a locked door or the boarded-up windows was sure to alert the occupants. Right behind him, he could feel Joe breathing down his neck. Then, suddenly, luck played in for them! A crack of light showed on the porch, revealing the door. A man's face appeared at the crack.

"Josef! Hans! What's keeping you?" the man called softly. "Hurry up. We've got to get out of here. Already we have wasted too much time." There was no answer to his inquiry. He stepped out on the porch, leaving the door cracked. "Hans!" he called softly. "That's queer. Wonder what . . ."

He never finished what he was wondering. Joe Beasley grabbed the agent by the ankle, dragging him off the porch into the sand. His frightened yell brought two FBI men on the run.

Like a flash, Big Jens was through the door of the kitchen, his service automatic drawn and ready. Right behind him swarmed plainclothes men and armed guards with drawn guns. The smell of gasoline was everywhere.

"Come out with your hands up," a guard yelled. "We've got you covered, and the house is surrounded!"

"Be careful," Big Jens called. "This place is likely to explode any minute."

The men tore through the old house searching, but they found no other enemy agents.

"There's a girl in this house somewhere," the chief shouted. "Taffy Willis is in here! Find her!"

He sped through a narrow corridor into a big room in the center of the house. Dim electric bulbs burned from two wall brackets, throwing a feeble light over wall and desk apparatus that looked for all the world like the radio room of a big battleship. Big Jens had found the answer all right!

"Some sweet little set-up," the skipper snarled, more angry than he had ever been in his whole life. Angry with himself for not having investigated that suspicious-looking object on the Snyder chimney when he first noticed it.

Then he saw Taffy!

She was lying quiet and still on the floor where the Nazi agents had left her. She was trussed up, the blindfold still over her eyes. A dark blanket was carelessly tossed on top of her. The odor of chloroform hung about her.

Big Jens knelt and listened to her heart. He felt her pulse.

"I've found her! She's alive!" Big Jens yelled exultantly. "Taffy, wake up, girl! It's Big Jens!" He untied the ropes, and with the help of Tom Stogner, the pharmacist's mate, he tried to help her up. But she was limp as a dishrag. He shook her. "Taffy, wake up," he commanded sternly. But Taffy was out cold.

"Let's get her into the fresh air, sir," Tom said,

rubbing her arms and legs to restore circulation.

"Get the jeep and some blankets," the skipper commanded. "And hurry. This girl's been drugged or something. Probably knocked on the head too, judging by this lump behind her ear. We've got to get her to the sickbay at the station . . . before it's too late. Call Ocracoke Base," he directed a guard, "and get Dr. Llewelyn over here as quick as possible. You boys knock out those windows. Let some air in the house. One of you take the truck and go get Gramp. Take him to the DF Station. Tell him Taffy's been thrown from her horse. I'll explain to him later."

In a matter of minutes Big Jens was settled in the jeep with Taffy held tenderly in his arms. "All right, fellows," he addressed his crew and the FBI men, "the rest of the party is yours. You can take it from here on in. I'm going to get this girl to the sickbay. Gun that motor, Joe, and don't let any grass grow under your wheels.

◆　◆　◆　◆　◆　◆　◆　◆

It was after midnight when Taffy awoke. Gramp sat by the side of the bed. Brandy squatted on his haunches, his nose on the white coverlet. Big Jens, a pharmacist's mate, and Dr. Llewelyn stood on the other side of the bed.

"She's coming out of it," the doctor told them. "She's got a nasty bump on the side of her head, but she'll be all right."

Taffy tried to move, but she was sore as a boil. Her head ached something awful and she was dreadfully sick at her stomach.

"Where am I?" she whispered weakly. "Where's Sailor? What place is this? How'd I get here?"

"You're at the DF Station. In the sickbay," Big Jens told her gently.

"I don't understand," she looked perplexed. "Where's my pony? He shied at something coming down the back road and threw me. Did I hit my head on a root or something? I can't remember. Happened close by the Snyder place. Last thing I remember was like I was being smothered to death."

Big Jens looked at the doctor and shook his head. Gramp wiped salt tears off his cheeks. "Sailor's home

in the lean-to," he told her. "When he came tearin'
home withaout you, Oi figgered that rascal had
throwed you. We went lookin' for you — me and
Brandy."

"You got a bad knock on that head of yours." The
doctor smiled. "Here, I want you to drink this orange
juice. Your grandfather and the chief think you
should stay down here at the station tonight and
maybe tomorrow. Just so we can watch you in case
that bump on your head should want to kick up a
little."

"Reckon I'll be all right." Taffy grinned weakly.
"Guess I'm kind of sleepy, though. Wonder what
made Sailor shy. What you reckon it was, Gramp?"

Big Jens shook his head violently at Gramp Morgan.

"Well," Gramp hesitated, "it moight have been
a varmint of some koind . . . deer maybe."

"Shucks," Taffy yawned, "Sailor isn't afraid of
those little toy deer. I just can't keep my eyes open,
I'm so sleepy."

"Well, we're going to leave you and let you sleep."
Big Jens grinned. "All of us except Brandy. Looks
as if we'd have to pry his nose loose off that bed-

spread. Brandy'll be as good a nurse as anybody, won't he, Doc?" Dr. Llewelyn nodded.

Gramp bent down and kissed Taffy's cheek. But she was sound asleep.

They all left the room.

"Whoy, she don't even know what she's been through or what happened to her," Gramp marveled.

"It's better that way, Gramp," Big Jens told him. "It will be better if she doesn't find out for a long, long time. As far as I know, Gramp Morgan, you are the only civilian on this island who knows what has happened tonight. Let's keep it that way. My crew are servants of Uncle Sam. So are the FBI men you saw. Catching enemy agents is part of our job. We are all sworn to secrecy. This war isn't over yet by a long shot. You have a double duty when it comes to silence . . . one to Taffy, and one to your country. Taffy's young, Gramp. There isn't any need to tell her about this night's business. It might do her irreparable harm. Just let her go on thinking that Sailor threw her. Nothing else, you understand?"

"Oi understand, Big Jens," Gramp Morgan said, solemnly shaking the chief's hand. "She'll not hear it from me. And Oi'll chew aout anybody else that dares mention it," Gramp told him sternly. "Loike Oi always say, what a body don't know, won't hurt them."

"Only this time, it nearly did," Big Jens thought grimly. "That's the spirit, Gramp," he told the old man. "Now come on to the chief's quarters. That's where you're going to sleep tonight. Right close to Taffy. Be sure to say your prayers . . . special ones tonight, Gramp Morgan. We'll all be able to sleep better on this island from now on, I'm thinking. And don't forget, every one of us owes Taffy, Malene, and Brandy a great debt of gratitude for getting that saboteur last night. Yeah, Gramp, tonight say some special prayers of thankfulness."

"Aye, and that Oi will," Gramp nodded solemnly, popping a quid of Brown's Mule into his jaw.